I0666242

My heart started thumping in my chest. I walked over to the costume jewelry counter and started to examine some bolo ties. No, too long and stringy. They'd be too hard to hide. Earrings. Yeah, they were just the thing. All I'd have to do was reach over and pick a card off the rack.

My eyes swept up and down the counter checking out where the salesgirl was. She'd turned her back. I looked around. No one else was looking. Then I looked up at the video surveillance camera overhead. I could see it moving slowly back and forth. Right now, the monitor was on the jeans rack.

Ready, set, NOW!

I darted my hand out.

BREAKING
All the Rules

Karle Dickerson

To Connie

Published by Willowisp Press, Inc.
401 E. Wilson Bridge Road, Worthington, Ohio 43085

Copyright©1990 by Willowisp Press, Inc.

All rights reserved. No portion of this book may be reproduced, stored in a retrieval system, or transmitted, in any form or by any means, electronic, mechanical, photocopying, recording or otherwise without prior written permission from the publisher.

Printed in the United States of America

10 9 8 7 6 5 4 3 2 1

ISBN 0-87406-474-0

One

"**W**HO cares if you just won the biggest diamond in the whole world? Do you have to stand there and kiss my mother like that on TV in front of everybody?" I yelled. "What a total gross out."

I pushed a button on the remote control and our wide-screen TV clicked off. I don't know why I had even turned on the TV to begin with. I don't watch much TV—and I hardly ever watch game shows. I especially don't watch *Treasure Trove*.

You might think that's kind of strange, since my mom is the star of the show. She's Desiree Sparks, the flashiest and most famous game-show hostess on TV. Most girls would be thrilled about having a TV star for a mom. I guess I'm different than your average 13 year old—to say the least.

I set down the remote control and put my

feet up on the seat in front of me. I checked out my new red shoes for a moment. Letting out a humongous sigh, I looked around in our darkened TV room and wondered what to do next. I was bored, bored, BORED. Mother probably wouldn't be home for hours. I think she had some publicity event to go to. I always lose track of those things. As for my stepdad, Alfred, forget it. He was on location somewhere. He's a movie producer. All that means is that he's never home. Then I thought of Sheila, our housekeeper. Maybe she'd think of something for me to do.

"Sheila," I called as I pressed the intercom button next to me. "Where are you?"

Sheila's voice came through the speaker. "Yes, Miss?"

"I'm bored," I said softly, even though I knew what Sheila would say.

"Did you do your homework yet, Miss?" Sheila asked.

"I can't," I said quickly. "I left all my books at school."

"Oh, your mother's not going to be pleased," Sheila said.

I didn't answer. I just clicked off the intercom and stood up. I walked out of the TV room and listened to my new shoes echo across the floor of the hallway. Catching a glimpse of myself in the mirror that hung in the entryway, I studied myself.

On the surface, I guess I should be happy. My blond hair is soft and catches lots of highlights. My face is okay. I mean, I like my blue eyes. My mouth is a little bit too full, but people say I'm as pretty as my mother. I'm tall and thin, but have some curves. As far as looks go, I get by.

And as far as brains go, I'm not stupid. I could make the honor roll if I wanted to. But I don't want to. I can act as well as my mom. But I never want to be on TV. I mean, why waste acting talent just to act goofy every day on TV where everyone can see you?

Walking up the winding staircase to my room, I asked myself the same question I'm always asking myself. If I have all these reasons to be happy, then why is my life so crummy? I lay back on my bed, thinking about how everything in my room matched—and how I always feel like the one who doesn't match anything else. I've been to at least six schools since kindergarten. I guess I've become kind of an expert at not fitting in. And just when I do start to fit in someplace, something happens and somebody at school tells my mom that "perhaps Lindsay would do better in another environment."

I jumped up, and just because no one was looking, I slid down the bannister. Then I slipped out the French doors in back. I walked up to our Great Dane, Duke, who was on watchdog duty out there. He let me scratch him under his chin for a minute, but then he lumbered off. "Great," I said to myself. "Even my dog doesn't have time for me."

I made my way back to the stables. We don't have horses, so Mother and Alfred, my stepdad, use the stables for gardening stuff. I use it to store the motor scooter that Mother bought me a few months ago. She buys me stuff when she feels sorry for me or guilty for working so much. She had felt sorry for me because I got kicked out of my private school. I had to start at a new school, a public one, Foothill Middle School. So she bought me the scooter.

I also like to come down to the stables to think. And I had nothing to do now but think. I sat down on the seat of the shiny red scooter, picked up a stick, and wrote my name in the dirt. Above my head was an old, splintery sign that said Princess. I think Princess was a horse that belonged to the people who used to live here.

I'd never been around animals much. But it occurred to me that it might be fun to have something like a horse to love. The thought made me crack up. I couldn't even picture my glamorous TV star mother getting near a horse, let alone having one in her backyard! I started to feel sad because I'd never be able to have a horse.

RRRRRRING!

The jangle of the phone in the stable startled me. I picked up the phone and chirped out a cheery hello. Whoever it was would never guess I was feeling blah.

"Oh, darling, it's Mother."

Mother's too-bright voice came through the phone. I knew that tone and gripped the phone tighter. It meant she was about to tell me something I wasn't going to like.

"You're not coming home until late again?" I asked.

"Surprise!" she answered. "I've sent William home with the car, and he's to take you to Rive Gauche. We'll have dinner together. I have another dreadful press event to go to afterward, but I did manage to pencil in dinner with my favorite daughter."

"Oh," I said, twisting the phone cord. I hate it when Mother squeezes me in—Lindsay: my 7:00 appointment. "Okay," I said in a little voice.

"Bye, bye, sweetheart. Kiss, kiss." Then

Mother hung up.

I went back in the house and up to my room. I looked into my closet at my clothes for a minute. Should I show up in sloppy jeans just to get on Mother's nerves? Nah, I decided. Instead I picked out a silky, royal blue shirtdress. I was putting on some big, dangly earrings that I knew Mother wouldn't like when I heard Sheila's voice on the intercom.

"William's ready for you."

"Coming," I yelled into the speaker.

I nodded at William as I slid into the back of our long, gray limousine. The leather seat felt lonely and cold. I wondered what Mother was going to dump on me this time. Leaning forward, I pressed the button that rolled down the glass partition that separated the back-seat from the front.

"Hey, William," I said, leaning over the seat. "Did you go to the Dodger game last night?"

William grinned. He loves baseball.

"Their best game this season!" he crowed as he took off his chauffeur's hat and waved it.

We talked baseball for a while. It did help me forget my blahs for a bit. I glanced at the car phone and wished I had someone to call. But I couldn't think of anyone I really wanted to talk to. I used to have this sort-of friend named Lisa Halloran. But we weren't speaking much these days. Too bad. She might have been a good friend. I just can't seem to get too close to people. When your mom is a big TV star, you never know when you might start talking too much. Saying things that you shouldn't say.

Like once, a few years ago, I told this nice lady about how my mom was so busy with her career, she never had time for me. Well, how was I supposed to know she was a writer for one of those celebrity-gossip magazines? The next day, the Valley Scoop Sheet ran the headline: "TV's Desiree Sparks Has No Time For Daughter. Poor Little Rich Girl Spills All!" Since then, I've learned to keep my mouth shut. It's easier that way. Except for the loneliness.

I picked up the car phone and fiddled with it for a while. I thought about calling Kevin, this guy in my drama class I sort of like. Then I decided against it. He's cute, but we don't seem to get along too well. Anyway, I wasn't sure if he even liked me, which was weird because, not to brag, people usually like me. Usually it's only because they want to be friends with a star's daughter. Holding the receiver button down, I talked into the mouthpiece to no one.

"Hello. Can you hear me? This is Lindsay. Lindsay Sparks. I'm bored, and I don't have anyone to talk to."

I waited for an imaginary voice to answer, then went on.

"Yeah. I know a TV star's daughter shouldn't get bored. After all, it's parties, parties, parties all the time, right?"

William looked at me in the rearview mirror.

"Are you okay?" he asked.

"Yeah," I laughed, feeling silly and hanging up the phone. "Hey, William. Next time you take your kids to the game, can I go along?"

"You bet," he said with a grin.

We pulled up in front of the fancy French restaurant Mother likes to go to. I hopped out without waiting for William to open the door for me.

"I'll save you some escargot in a napkin," I said with a wink. It was our joke. William hates fancy food—particularly snails.

"Give me a Dodger dog anytime," he said.

I walked slowly up the front steps. I threw back my shoulders, tilted up my chin and gave my best dazzling smile to the maitre d' as he held the door. After all, I was in public now.

And it was show time.

"Good evening, Mademoiselle. Madame Desiree is waiting," he said in a French accent.

"Ah, very good," I said, stealing a line from a play I'd once been in.

I followed the maitre d' toward the back of the restaurant where Mother always sits so she won't be recognized. A couple of people turned and looked at me, but suddenly I didn't want to play showtime anymore. I just wished I was an ordinary kid with a mom who worked in a grocery store.

"There you are, sweetheart," murmured Mother as she stood up and gave me a silky, perfumy hug.

"Motherrr," I whined. "This is embarrassing."

My mother sniffed and sat down.

"Can't a mother show a little affection for her daughter?" she asked.

I slid into my chair. We sat there in silence while the waiter poured water. I watched my mother shift around in her seat. It seemed like she was searching for something to say. I didn't want to make it any easier on her. I dipped my finger into my water glass and ran it around on the rim to see if it would make a humming noise, just to bug her.

She frowned. "Lindsay, dear, please."

I sighed and wiped my finger on the pink linen napkin. "Okay," I said. "What's up?"

Mother sat there for a moment, toying with the tassel on the menu. "Let's order first," she finally said. "And how was your day at school?"

"What's this all about?" I asked.

"Lindsay, sweetheart, I don't want it to be like this," she began.

"Like what?"

"Lindsay, I asked about your day."

"I had a normal day, just like every other day," I answered. "What's going on?"

She took a deep breath. "All right, I'll tell you. Lindsay, your stepfather and I—"

I winced and she stopped. Mother looked at her hand and I realized she wasn't wearing her sapphire wedding ring.

"—what I'm trying to say is, Alfred and I—we need time apart."

"Oh," I said in a small voice. "But I was just starting to like Alfred. Just when I start to get used to them, they're gone."

Mother looked at me and went on in a rush. "I've been very upset about all this, and the producer said I could take a few weeks off. I need to get away. I've booked a flight for Paris. I leave in a couple of days."

"And what about me?" My voice sounded

weird, even to me.

Mother reached across the table to take my hand. I pulled it away and took a gulping breath. I felt like someone had kicked me in the stomach. I wouldn't cry—not in front of her. Lindsay's law.

"Honey, I promise I'll make it up to you. I really will."

"How? What will you buy me?" I asked.

"We'll get together just as soon as I get back. Maybe take a little vacation together. Or maybe we could fly to New York again soon? In the meantime, is there anything I can do?" Mother asked, looking hopeful.

"How about buying me a horse?" I asked impulsively, just to see if she'd do it.

Mother blinked. "I didn't know you wanted a horse. You know I'd buy you anything that would make you happy, but a horse?"

"Oh, just forget the horse," I burst out. "I can't believe you're getting another divorce. And I don't want you to leave and—"

And I want you to have a normal life and let me have one, too! I thought.

"Look, I didn't plan any of this, sweetheart, and it's hard on me, too," Mother said. "Anyway, I didn't say divorce. I meant a sort of...separation. And I was just trying to think of something nice to do for you. We'll talk about this more later. Look, here comes the waiter. Do you know what you want to order?"

On the way home, I kept the partition up in our car. William must have known I was crying, but he didn't say anything as he opened the door. I climbed out slowly, my body feeling like a wet bag of cement. Sheila opened the front door and rested her hand on my shoulder. She must have known what was going on. I shook her hand off my shoulder and dragged my way up to my room.

Moonlight was spilling onto my floor through the window. I slumped into a ball right in the middle of the moonlit spot and looked out at the tall pines rustling outside my window.

How many times have I been told about what a glamorous exciting life I lead? *Hey, Lindsay. What's it like to be a TV star's daughter?* I've been asked that at least four bezillion times.

"It's the pits!" I shouted into the darkness of my room. "I hate it!"

But there was no one who really mattered in our big, beautiful house to hear me.

Two

SO that was that. A few days later, Mother took the Concorde to Paris. I took my motor scooter to Foothill Middle School to face another day. Oh, you wouldn't have noticed anything was wrong by looking at me. I never give anything away. The worse I feel, the wilder I dress. Lindsay's law.

That morning, I'd put on a ton of lip gloss and painted my nails with a different color of nail polish on each nail. Then I pushed aside what Sheila had set out for me to wear. Instead, I wore one of my favorite outfits, a long, shocking pink sweater that reached almost to my knees, and my acid-washed jeans. I could almost get lost in that sweater. I had to keep shoving up the sleeves as I zipped along the streets on my scooter.

When I turned into the driveway by the bike rack at school, I looked around to see if any kids I knew were there—yep—right by the flagpoles as always. I waved at them, jumped up the curb, and zipped right toward them on the sidewalk.

"Lindsay!" shouted Lori Pendleton, jumping back. She's pretty, popular—and I like her okay. She is totally impressed by me—the almost-star. Actually, she's so into herself that she never tries to get too close. She follows Lindsay's law when it comes to making friends.

"I thought you weren't supposed to ride that thing to school anymore," said Maria Perez.

I shrugged and switched off the motor. Then I climbed off, walking the scooter right up next to her. "I'm not riding it. I'm walking it," I said.

"Tell that to Ms. Sheldon," said Maria with a lopsided smile.

Ms. Sheldon—the principal—and I do not get along. Especially not after I wrote her phone number in the boys' bathroom a couple of weeks ago.

"Big news," said Lori, forgetting about my scooter. "Big party in a couple of weeks at Kevin Hiller's house. It's for the drama club, but other people can go, too."

I raised my eyebrows. I don't really like

parties all that much, but I kind of had my eye on Kevin, like I said before. I didn't belong to the drama club, even though I had been in some school plays. I don't like clubs. But I was hoping that Kevin would ask me. His party would be the perfect thing to help me forget that my mother had just broken up with husband number three, and left me alone with a housekeeper.

To try to fight the tears that were ready to come to my eyes, I said loudly, "Can't wait! I live to party!"

"Don't look now, but here comes Lisa Halloran," Maria said.

I looked up as Lisa walked past me, talking with her best friend, Bev Hansen. My heart gave a funny jolt just then, but I simply rolled my eyes.

"YAWN," I said loudly for effect, though I kind of hoped Lisa didn't hear. I wasn't about to let anyone see how much it hurt me that Lisa and I weren't friends anymore.

There were lots of people who would have said it was all my fault. But things weren't that simple. You see, I liked her brother, Ash, a lot. And I liked Lisa a lot, too. But it didn't take too long to see that Ash and Lisa, well, they were different. They were getting too close to me, almost like a brother and a sister.

It was too scary. So I pretended not to like them anymore. And since I'm a good actress, everybody believed that I really didn't like them.

Just then the bell rang. We all piled into the building. Standing in front of my locker, I felt someone tap me on the shoulder. I turned around slowly, tilting my head and waving my blond hair back in case it was someone important.

It was. Kevin was standing there, looking totally cute. He was tall, with dark hair. Sometimes—like right then—it was hard to remember he made me furious on a regular basis in drama class. Most of the time, he was the basic babe of my dreams.

"Greetings, earthling," I said, stealing a line from one of our last scenes together. It wasn't easy to act like his being so close to me didn't give me a giant-sized case of the knee shakes.

"Hi, Lindsay," Kevin said. "I just wanted to tell you I got the early report on drama class. Thought you deserved a warning—Mr. Mosely stuck us together for a scene again. It's due in a couple of weeks."

"You're kidding!" I exclaimed. Kevin looked hurt at that. He shifted his books into his other hand and looked at the ground.

"Look, I know you think I'm a total zero and

that I can't act nearly as well as you can—" he started to say.

"Aw, come on. Lighten up," I said quickly. "I didn't mean it that way. It's just that well, you know. Whenever we do stuff together in class, we end up fighting all the time."

"I know," Kevin said. "But if we're stuck doing this scene together, let's try to make the best of it."

Why was I in drama in the first place? Mother wouldn't hear of my transferring out. And Kevin drove me crazy with his nonstop self-confidence. I just faked mine, but his was the real thing. And sometimes it made me mad.

Kevin held up one hand in surrender. "Okay. Okay. But we'd better call a truce if we're going to get a good grade on this next scene. I need a good grade. So do you."

I nodded my head. He was right about that.

"And act like you're surprised when Mosely announces it in class," Kevin called out as he started down the hall. "No one's supposed to know."

"Oh, great," I muttered to myself. As if I didn't have enough hassles with Mother separating from Alfred and leaving me at home while she jetted off to Paris. Now I had to do another scene with Kevin. If we kept getting stuck in scenes together and fighting with each other, he'd never get to like me. I'd always be Lindsay, that girl he always fought with.

I did my best to get through that day. The only thing that seemed real was the humongous hurt inside me that just seemed to get bigger and bigger. As soon as school was out, I knew I'd have to go home to an empty house with an empty stable. Even Princess, a stupid horse I'd never met, had left.

Okay, so Mother wouldn't buy me a horse. Well, who said I couldn't buy *myself* something. I decided I'd go to the mall and buy myself a lot of somethings. Sneaking a look into my purse, I saw that I had a couple of the credit cards that Mother let me sign on. That's it, I thought. I'll buy myself something outrageous for Kevin's party.

When the final bell rang, I zipped out the door and pushed my way through the crowded halls. I'd have to call William to pick me up. No way was I taking the scooter to the mall. And forget walking. I never walk anywhere. Lindsay's law.

I dropped a quarter into the pay phone and pushed the buttons. While I waited for an answer, I turned around and watched people walk by. Most of them waved at me. I waved and smiled back. But when Lisa Halloran and

22

Bev Hansen walked by, I didn't wave or smile. Bev looked right past me, but Lisa slowed a little. Was she going to say something? She looked right at me, but just then, Sheila picked up the phone, and I turned my back to Lisa.

"Sheila, it's me. Please have William come pick me up. I want to go shopping," I said.

"Homework first, Miss," Sheila said.

"Done already. During study hall," I lied. Actually, I had a stupid essay to write for English tonight as well as practicing the scene for drama. Just then, I noticed Bev had dropped a piece of notebook paper.

"Well, if you're sure," Sheila sighed.

"Sure I'm sure," I said, hanging up.

I walked over and picked up the paper that must have dropped out of Bev's notebook. It was a note Lisa had written to Bev about some class assignment. She'd signed it *LYLAS*.

I frowned, trying to remember what that meant. Oh, yeah. It meant *Love Ya Like A Sister*. We'd all signed our yearbooks last spring at my other school like that. I'd sign *Love Ya Like A Sister, Lindsay*. I realized that I didn't know anyone at this school that I'd write *LYLAS* to.

Just then a group of kids walked by—I didn't know any of them. They all looked at me and one of the kids pointed and whispered something to the rest of the group.

"TV star," was all I heard. Their heads all collected together and moved down the hall in one giggling, happy glob.

Suddenly, I felt really tired. Tired of always being on show. Tired of being hassled about doing my homework. Tired of feeling alone. Most of all I was tired of being the Famous TV Star's Daughter.

I wadded up the note and tossed it in the trash can. I reached down and felt the credit cards in my purse.

Watch out, shopping mall. Here comes Lindsay.

Three

WILLIAM dropped me off in front of "Super Sock." It was this cute little store right next to the entrance that sold only socks. It was as good a place to start as any, I decided.

"Can I help you?" this strange-looking salesgirl asked me. She was wearing these lime green checkered anklets. That was nothing. I could outdo her any day.

"Yeah," I said. "I want a few dozen pairs of socks. All different colors. Do you have any mismatched ones?"

The girl blinked. "A—few dozen?" she sputtered. "Mismatches?"

I ignored her and glided past, staring at the socks displayed on the wall. I chose about 20 pairs, ripped open the packages, and just took one of each sock to the counter. Some of the socks on display had little plastic animals and designs pinned on them. I'd seen them in magazines, but nobody at my school wore them. Maybe it was time to start a new trend.

"Sock charms," I said. "I want all the weirdest ones." I picked out a few packages of tarantulas, armadillos, snakes, trash cans, typewriters, and these great little iguanas.

As I watched her ring up the socks and charms, I realized that I'd always hated pairs of things. Things don't come in pairs in my life. Like me—I don't feel like I go with anything.

"Wow," said the salesgirl, handing me my bag. "Twenty pairs of socks at one time. You sure are lucky!"

"Lucky?" I repeated, thinking of my empty house. "That's my middle name."

I felt a bit better walking out with my package. I laughed as I wondered what the salesgirl was going to do with all the mateless socks I'd left behind. I hit a couple more stores after that, buying things and each time signing credit card slips. Maybe if I charged a lot of stuff, it would cause an alarm to go off in some credit card computer somewhere. Then they'd have to call my mom in Paris. And if they did, maybe I could talk to her. Ouch. I really missed her.

I bought two new pairs of jeans, some hair

accessories, eight different lipsticks in all different shades of pink, and two long T-shirts that said "Catch me if you can." But I didn't find anything to wear to Kevin's party.

Soon I was carrying so many bags, I couldn't carry any more. It was time to hit the fast-food court and sit down for a while. I headed right to the escalator, then down to Oh! Egg Roh!lls, my favorite place. Plunking my bags down at a table in front of it, I went over to the counter and got three egg rolls and a soda.

"Check it out. Look at all those bags," said a voice right behind me.

I turned around slowly. Three girls I'd never seen before were standing by the table I'd set my bags down on. They were all dressed in black jeans and black sweaters. Bor-RING, I thought. Why did they all dress alike?

When they saw me looking at the bags, they stepped back and looked back at me.

"Those all yours?" one girl with short, dark hair asked me. Her eyes slid over me. It was the same kind of look I give people when I want them to think I'm cool. I've practiced it in front of my mirror at least a bezillion times.

I shrugged. "Could be."

The three looked at each other.

"This is our mall. We always check out who hangs here," the tallest girl said. She shoved her hands in her pockets.

I picked up my egg rolls and tried not to laugh. No one owned a mall. Anyone could hang out at a mall. Lindsay's law.

"Check it out all you want," I said, marching over to my table. I sat down by my bags.

The tall girl came over and sat on the table. I sipped my soda, but didn't say anything. I could see Tall Girl eyeing my fingernails. I drummed them on the table so she could see that I had a different color on each nail.

"Go ahead. Open up the packages," I said to the other girls, who were still looking at all my bags. I did have an impressive collection. Anyway, I didn't want them to think I was scared of them, though they were starting to make me feel a little uncomfortable.

"Socks? Just socks?" the dark-haired girl said as she poked her nose into the first bag.

"Go ahead. Have a few," I said. I don't know why I said it. Maybe they'd go away if I gave them something. And I could definitely spare a few socks that day. They looked like the types who'd like mismatched socks anyway.

"How about an egg roll instead?" Tall Girl asked, looking at my plate.

I reached into my purse and pulled out a $5 bill. "I'm hungry. Go buy your own," I said, flicking the bill at Tall Girl.

She jumped up. "We don't want your money, rich girl," she snapped.

Then Quiet One, who I really hadn't noticed before, said, "Aw, chill out, J.J. She's just being nice. Besides, I'm hungry."

J.J. looked at her friend and said, "Okay, Robbie. Go get some egg rolls."

Pretty soon Quiet One came back with the egg rolls and a large soda to share. The three girls sat at my table and started to chat while they ate. And actually, I started to have a good time. The girls were pretty funny.

It turned out these three girls went to a school across town and were in the eighth grade, just like me. But they cut even more school than I did. And they hung out at the mall—every day.

"That's right—every day," said Quiet One.

"Certified Mall Rats," said Short Hair proudly. I found out her name was—get this— Lisa.

I shook my head. I thought I was outrageous, but these girls had definitely outdone me. "I don't get it," I said. "What do you do at this boring old mall all the time?"

The three looked at each other and smiled. They weren't about to let me in on their secrets. I was too new—the rich girl.

Then two thoughts struck me at the same

time. One, I wanted these girls to like me and let me in on their secrets. Two, they couldn't ever know I was Desiree Sparks' daughter. You see, I'd figured them out right away. They were bad girls. And they'd never want anything to do with me if they figured out who I was. They were way too cool to be impressed by a celebrity's daughter.

"We play video games at the arcade," Lisa said.

"Where are you from?" asked J.J. "What's your name?"

"Olivia," I said quickly. Well, it wasn't exactly a lie. Olivia's my middle name. Actually, it was Mother's name too, before she changed it to Desiree.

"Olivia. Pretty name," said Robbie. She took another bite out of her egg roll.

No one asked about last names. And they also didn't ask any more questions. That was fine with me. It was safer that way. Lisa Halloran would probably have asked me a bezillion questions by now. *How did I feel about my mom's newest separation. How I was feeling about being left behind.* Who needed friends like that?

J.J. licked her fingers. "Well, Olivia, what's next?"

I didn't want the girls to go away. I didn't

feel like being alone just then. "How about going to play some video games?" I suggested.

"Naw. No money," said Lisa.

"No problem," I said, reaching into my purse and pulling out another $5 bill.

"Let's go," said Robbie, jumping up.

J.J. held back. I could see I made a mistake. I was going to be labeled rich girl forever if I wasn't careful.

I knew what to say. "I swiped this money, from—someone I know," I lied.

J.J. must have thought this was the right answer. "Okay," she said. "Let's go play video games."

We got up and walked out of the food court. Robbie stopped to look at something in the window. I glanced at my watch. William would be out in front of the entrance waiting for me by now. And there was no way I was going to let my new friends see me get into a limousine. After we'd played a few games, I'd have to slip out the other entrance. And, much as I hated walking, I'd have to walk home.

We started toward the escalator. The three girls rushed in front of me, accidentally sideswiping an older lady. She dropped one of her shopping bags. The girls started laughing. Without thinking, I stopped, picked up the bag, handed it to the lady, and apologized.

The lady glared at my new friends, then gave me a smile. "Thank you, dearie. You're a good girl."

"Olivia, Certified Good Girl," J.J. said out loud as she and Lisa stepped onto the escalator.

"Thank you, dearie," added Lisa, imitating the lady.

The woman shook her head and walked past all of us.

"Let's find the emergency button that shuts down the escalator," hissed Robbie as I stepped off at the top.

J.J. thought about it, but decided against it.

"Naw," she said, motioning in my direction. "We don't want Olivia to think we're bad girls, now do we?"

The others thought that was hysterically funny. They laughed and laughed. I pretended it went right over my head. The time would come when I would show them just what kind of girl Olivia was.

Lindsay, the Certified Good Girl, the one who played by the rules and lost anyway, was gone. I followed my new friends toward the video arcade. Look out, world, you haven't messed with Olivia yet!

Four

WALKING home from the mall was a big mistake! My shopping bags were heavy. By the time I got home, my arms felt like they were going to fall off. I ditched one of the bags in some bushes in front of my house. I didn't want Sheila to see how much stuff I had. She'd probably go nutzoid.

I really wished I could slip in unnoticed, but there was no way. We have this security system, and from the outside, I couldn't buzz myself in. So I had to press the button. Sheila buzzed through the intercom, "Yes, may I help you?"

"It's Oli—Lindsay," I said impatiently. Oops—I almost slipped.

The buzzer sounded, and I let myself in through the gate, then lugged my bags up the walk.

Sheila opened the front door, and crossed

33

her arms in front of her chest.

"William was waiting for you. Where were you?" she demanded.

"You're not my mother," I snapped back. Then I felt bad right away. I mean, Sheila was usually pretty okay to me. It really wasn't right to take things out on her.

"Okay," I said. "I stayed too long at the mall, and I...uh decided to walk home," I said in a nicer voice.

Sheila looked at my bags. "You never walk anywhere. And now you're telling me you wanted to walk home when you had all those bags to carry?"

I stepped inside the door and put the bags down. "Aw, they weren't heavy. There aren't so many bags," I mumbled.

"How did you pay for all those things?"

"Charge cards," I said. "No big deal."

Sheila frowned. "You're not supposed—"

"Well, I did. So what?" Here I was trying to be nice to her and she was giving me all this grief.

"I think I should call your mother," Sheila said.

"Good. Go ahead. Tell on me," I yelled.

Sheila sighed and shook her head. She turned to walk toward Mother's office.

"By the way, your stepfather called from

Atlanta. And he sent you some flowers. And you had a phone call from a young man named Kevin," she said.

"Oh," I said casually, ignoring the part about Alfred. I was wondering how Kevin got my phone number. It's no big surprise that Desiree Sparks has an unlisted number.

"Did Kevin leave his number?" I asked, grabbing a couple of bags and starting up the stairs.

"Yes. I wrote it down for you." She handed me a piece of paper. When I got to my room, I tossed the bags down and reached for the phone. Then I dialed. I hoped that his mother or someone didn't answer the phone. I flopped down on my bed and flipped my shoes off. Ouch, my feet were sore, sore, sore!

"Hello." Bingo—Kevin's voice answered.

"Hi, it's Lindsay. You called?"

"Yeah. I was just wondering if I, uh, could come over and maybe we could start to work on our scene together?" Kevin asked. "That is, if you're not busy or anything."

I sat up and clutched the phone. The old uneasiness came crashing back on me like a giant wave. I don't know why, but I have this thing about people coming over to my house. I don't think I've ever had people over here. Except Lisa. Once. And I think that was a big mistake. I mean, it's one thing for people to know your mother's a TV star. It's another thing when they actually see the way we live. It kind of blows them away, and it makes me feel weird. I definitely didn't want Kevin feeling weird around me.

"Uh, I'm not busy," I said quickly. "But how about if we just meet somewhere—like the conference room at the library or—or something?"

Kevin started laughing. "Lindsay, do you even know where the library is?"

That made me mad. "Yes! I do!" I said, accenting each word. Two minutes into a phone conversation, and Kevin and I were already arguing. See what I mean?

"Sorry," Kevin said. "That wasn't very nice. It's just that I can't picture you at a library."

Actually, I went to the library a lot, mostly to check out videos of classic movies. But I wasn't about to let Kevin in on my secret. Since our library's so close to all the TV studios, it has this huge entertainment section. My favorites were the old black and white movies with the old-time stars.

Kevin apologized again. "Okay, let's meet at the library."

I agreed to meet him there in a half-hour and hung up the phone. Now the problem was

36

convincing Sheila to let me go. After all, I'd gotten her mad and hadn't even eaten dinner.

This would take a big-time acting job. No biggie—I could pull it off. I was a good actress.

I walked into my closet. Way in the back (I didn't wear this kind of stuff very often), I found a plain white blouse and a navy pleated skirt. Just right for a schoolgirl look. I put my hair into a low ponytail and took off my huge earrings. Then I put them back on because I decided Sheila would suspect something if I looked too different.

I walked down the staircase, slowly getting into my part—The Apologetic Girl. Then I laughed as I thought about J.J. If only she could see me now! Well, I better wipe the smile off my face and get into my part. I quickly thought of my mother being gone, and that made me stop smiling in a hurry. By the time I walked into the dining room, where Sheila was supervising the maid who was serving dinner, my face looked so sad it would have broken your heart.

"I'm sorry that I made you worry and that I acted so rotten to you," I said. I lowered my eyes. Even so, I could feel Sheila's gaze burn through the top of my head.

"Look up at me," she said, tilting my chin with her finger.

I jerked away and looked down again. "Look, I said I'm sorry. I think I'd better skip dinner and head over to the library and try to finish my homework," I said. "I might as well try to get my grades up while Mother's gone."

I looked up then to see Sheila's reaction. No go. Her eyes pierced through me.

"Oh, Lindsay, what are you up to now?" she asked with a sigh.

"Nothing. I said I was sorry, and I want to go to the library and do my homework. What's wrong with that?" I asked.

Sheila turned away and started fussing with the flower arrangement on the long dining room table.

"You're playing games with me, young lady, and I won't have it," she said. "You told me you'd already done your homework when you called and asked to go to the mall. Now, you're going to stick around here this evening and that's that."

I could feel my cheeks flame. Usually I was too smart to forget an earlier lie. How embarrassing to get caught! Then I got mad. I wanted to go to the library. I wanted to see Kevin. And I couldn't call him back and tell him I couldn't go. He'd probably already left the house. But one look at Sheila told me she wasn't budging on this one.

I threw myself into my chair and noticed my place was the only one set. How dumb— the whole table was decked out with silver candlesticks and stuff, and I was the only one eating.

"Am I the only one eating?" I yelled. "Doesn't anyone in this stupid house want to eat with me?"

"Lindsay, be a good girl. I have some work to do. I'll put your mother's bell here and you may ring when you're ready to have the table cleared. Then perhaps I can join you for dessert." Sheila was nicer now. Maybe she was feeling sorry for me. Normally, that would make me mad, but tonight I zoomed in on it.

"After dinner, can I go to the library?" I asked one more time.

"No," Sheila answered. "We'll have no more of this conversation, if you please." She left the room.

I sat down and picked at the food the maid brought in. But when I was finished, I didn't ring the bell for the maid to clear the table. Instead, I slid out of my chair and slipped out the back door. I stomped over to the gardening shed and sat down in front of Princess' stall.

"Can you believe Sheila wouldn't let me go to the library?" I whispered to the horse that wasn't there.

There was no answer.

"Well, we were actually going to study," I whispered again. "Maybe I should sneak out anyway. Then Sheila will call my mother."

I brightened at the thought for a minute, but then wiped it out of my mind. Come to think of it, a trans-Atlantic argument with my mother wasn't really my idea of fun.

It was so lonely in that empty stable. I missed Princess, a horse I'd never seen. I missed my mother, and even my stepfather. Great big gulpy sobs filled me, and I had a great big feel-sorry-for-Lindsay cry-a-thon.

After a while, I got tired of crying. I wiped my eyes on the sleeve of my white blouse and wondered what Kevin would think when I didn't show up at the library. Well, too bad, I thought. People hurt my feelings all the time. Olivia was too tough to care.

I stuck my chin up the way I'd seen J.J. do, and walked back into the house and up to my room. I ignored Sheila when she came by to say good night.

The next day, I got up and dressed all in black. I wore a mismatched pair of socks and pinned my sock charms on. Olivia's first day of school. Sheila gave me funny look, but didn't say anything. I tossed down some orange juice and waited out front for William to pull the car up.

"Will you drop me off a block away from school?" I asked him as I slid into the back-seat. Olivia wasn't going to be seen driving up in a limo.

"Sorry, Miss. I take my orders from your mother. At school it is," William said.

"Please?" I asked, giving my widest smile.

He hesitated. Good. It was working.

"Okay. We'll compromise. How about if I drop you off just outside the gate?" William asked. "Then you can walk in."

When we got to school, William stopped the car just outside the gate. I jumped out with-out waiting for him to open the door for me. Turning around to wave, I walked through the gate to school. I spotted my friends by the flagpole and walked slowly up to them. Maria was the first to comment about my new look. "Check it out," she said to the other girls. "Lindsay's wearing black."

I shrugged. "So what?"

"It makes you look...well, tough," said Maria. I thought of my friends at the mall and smiled.

"I like your sock charms," Lori said. "Where

41

did you get them?" I stuck my foot out for everyone to see. I knew that by tomorrow, Lori and Maria and some of the others would have new sock charms of their own. And that thought made me laugh. Because then in a few days, I'd tell everyone that I thought sock charms were dumb and everyone would have to stop wearing them.

I was just about to tell everyone where I got them when I felt a tap on my shoulder. I turned around. It was Kevin.

"Where were you last night?" he asked. His eyes traveled over my black outfit.

I was ready to explain the whole thing, that Sheila wouldn't let me go, that I couldn't call because he would have already left. But I could feel everyone around watching, wide-eyed, and interested. There was no way I could admit in front of everyone what really happened. I was tough, right? I thought fast.

"I'm so sorry," I said, letting my voice rise in a wail. "But, you see, my dog—his name's Duke—got real sick suddenly, and I had to sit with him and wait till the veterinarian called us back and..."

Kevin looked like he didn't believe me, but he nodded his head. "Sorry about your dog. But we've got to get to work on our scene. We'll talk about it in class," he said, walking off.

I watched his back for a moment, feeling bad that I had had to lie to Kevin. But then I became Olivia again, and she didn't feel bad anymore. I decided to play Olivia to the fullest—tough, like nothing hurt me. Like it was no big deal that my life was exploding like a water balloon.

English class was a total bore. While someone was reading a stupid poem about feelings, I took off a couple of my sock charms and made them chase each other across my desk. This made the kids around me laugh, so Mr. Powers made me go to the principal's office.

While I sat in the outer office waiting for Ms. Sheldon to see me, Lisa Halloran walked by. We were the only two there, so she had to say something.

"Hi," she said.

Was she afraid of me? I wondered suddenly. It made me feel...well, kind of ashamed. I didn't know why. I wasn't used to feeling ashamed.

"How's it going?" I mumbled. I sort of smiled.

She brightened and stopped. Her hands fumbled with a button on her sweater.

"My mom said to say hello if I ever ran into you," she said shyly.

43

That was weird. I would have thought that Mrs. Halloran would hate me after the way Lisa and I stopped being friends. But she told Lisa to say hi to me? I didn't know what to say. So I shrugged. Then I threw back my head and looked at the ceiling. Lisa walked on.

Ms. Sheldon lectured me about causing trouble, and asked if there was anything I wanted to talk about. I smiled and told her everything was fine. She gave me a slip to go back to class and told me to behave or I'd be in real trouble.

Later that day, I went to drama class. Kevin acted pretty cold to me. So I acted cold back. We agreed on the scene we were going to do together—without a fight. It was from one of Mr. Moseley's one-act playbooks. Our scene was a dialogue between a pirate and a captive princess.

When class was over, Kevin didn't say anything about getting together for another study date. He just slapped his playbook closed and threw it in his backpack.

"Later," he said over his shoulder as he left the room.

Great. Now he was really mad, and he'd never invite me to his party. It made me feel depressed, so finally, I decided to cut seventh period and head over to the mall. Maybe my new friends would be there.

I hung out in the restroom right after sixth period and waited for the bell to ring. As soon as everyone cleared out, I slipped away from school unnoticed. I was on my way to the mall, ugh—walking again.

Sure enough, I saw J.J., Robbie, and Lisa leaning up against the wall by the food court. I waved when I saw them.

"Hi," they said, sounding bored.

I yawned. "What's going on?" I asked.

"Nothing," said Robbie. "We've been here all day. Where've you been?"

"Oh," I said with a shrug. "Nowhere special." I wasn't about to tell them I had been at school.

We hit the video arcade—my treat. Then we bought bubble gum and practiced cracking it until it echoed around the mall. J.J. jiggled the pay phones until a couple of quarters came out. We all chipped in with that and bought a soda to split at a fast-food place.

Just as we walked away from the counter, I looked up and saw Lisa Halloran heading right toward us. I couldn't believe how I kept bumping into her today. She was alone and carrying a "J. Bookworm" bag, reading a book while she was walking.

Just as she passed me, she looked up. I saw

her look at me quickly with surprise. Then her eyes darted to the other girls. Then she looked down quickly and passed us. But I could see what she was thinking loud and clear—losers.

That thought made me mad. Who was Lisa Halloran to label us? After all, she had everything: a picture-perfect family, a neat big brother like Ash, a mom who said hi to people who didn't deserve it, a normal home. Her mother didn't go jetting off to Paris and leave her behind—not like Lindsay—not like Olivia.

Lindsay's eyes prickled with tears, but Olivia said loudly to her new friends, "Check out the bookworm."

I felt Lisa's hurt as she turned and walked away. But Olivia just laughed with her new friends.

Five

WHEN I got home from the mall just before dinner, Sheila was waiting for me at the gate. "Where were you?" she asked.

"At the mall," I said as I passed her and went up the walk. She followed close behind.

"Now don't get smart with me. You didn't tell anyone where you were going. I've just put a call in to your mother," Sheila announced. "She should be calling back at any minute. You two have some things to discuss."

I shrugged, but smiled inside. Good, at least I'd get a chance to talk with my mom. Yeah, she'd probably get all mad at me for a while, but then she'd calm down, and I could talk with her. Wow, I missed her!

The phone rang just as we got inside the house. I made a beeline over to Mother's office, closed the door and picked up the phone. I plopped down at her expensive

Italian writing desk.

"Hello. To whom am I speaking?" It was Desiree's voice. Even through the hiss of the long-distance connection, I could hear her clearly. I played with some flowers that were in a crystal vase on the desk.

"It's your troublesome child," I said. "Olivia." I tried my new name out on her and snapped off the heads of a couple of flowers.

"Olivia? What's going on, Lindsay? Why are you calling yourself Olivia?" Desiree asked.

"I'm sick of Lindsay," I said. "How's Paris?"

"Lindsay is a beautiful name, dear—oh, never mind. Paris is fine. But Lindsay, what's going on there?" she asked. "Sheila tells me you—"

"Nothing's going on here. It's no big deal. I went to the mall this afternoon, and Sheila freaked because I forgot to tell her. That's all," I said. Then I shredded some leaves off the stems.

"Well, you simply must tell people where you are. I worry about you," Mother said.

"If you're so worried about me, then why are you in Paris, and why did you leave me here?" I yelled. Duke, who was lying in front of the fireplace, got up and lumbered out of the room. He hates arguments.

Mother started talking loudly, so I pulled

the phone away from my ear and stared at the walls instead of listening. I studied a couple of photos that were hanging by the desk of Desiree Sparks, the star. A big fake smile was pasted on her face. Desiree was accepting some award. Desiree was hugging some stupid contestant. Desiree was on the set of her stupid game show. Why didn't she use her acting talents in some good way? My mother gave away ridiculous stuff like his 'n' her llamas on national TV. For that, people called her a star.

"Lindsay, are you listening?" Mother's voice cut back in on me.

"Yeah, yeah," I muttered, putting the receiver to my mouth again.

"As I was saying, no more charges until I get back," Mother said. "If you need anything, let Sheila know. Anyway, I'll bring you back lots of presents. Now, Princess, I need to say good-bye."

I gripped the phone tighter. I didn't want her to go. Just hearing her voice made me feel better than I had in days. I tried to think of anything that might stall her for just a minute longer. Princess, she'd called me. That was a horse's name.

"Don't bring me any presents back unless you bring a horse," I said.

There was silence on the other end of the phone. Uh, oh, I'd really made Mother mad now. Good, I was glad she was mad.

"Lindsay, dear," she said after a moment, "You aren't serious about this horse business, are you?"

I started crying then. "I don't know," I said. "I don't care about the presents, just come back soon."

"Soon as I can, baby," she said. "I know that this is hard on you. I really do miss you."

And then she hung up.

I sat in Mother's office for awhile after that and doodled on her memo pad with a red pen. Why couldn't I have a normal family with a mother and father, a brother and sister, a family like, well, like Lisa's? It's really stupid to wish for things you could never have. I blobbed red ink on my nails and totally blottoed my polish.

The next morning, I painted over my nails in bright yellow polish. I ignored the clothes Sheila had set out for me and put on my black jeans and a black sweatshirt with silver studs on it. I dressed slowly so I wouldn't have time to eat. I didn't want Sheila lecturing me today at breakfast.

I watched myself in the gold gilt mirror walking down our winding staircase. I liked the way I looked in black. I looked unapproachable, untouchable, tough. "Don't touch me," I whispered to Olivia's reflection.

"You look serious today," William said when I climbed into the car.

"I feel serious," I said.

"You forgot your school books," Sheila said, running out to give them to me.

"Thanks," I said. I'd forgotten them on purpose. I didn't want to think of how behind I was getting at school. Anyway, I had my playbook for drama in my purse. That was all I needed. Our car slithered down the driveway, through the gate and out onto the street.

"What's going on at school today?" William asked brightly.

"Nothing, school is boring," I muttered, fiddling with the electric windows—up, down, up, down.

"There are no such things as boring places, only bored people," William said. "Think about it. You only get out of something what you put in."

I rolled my eyes and stuck out my tongue. But William couldn't see me. "I'll remember that, William," I said as we pulled up by the front gate of school. Of course, I planned to forget it right away.

I shoved my books under the seat after

checking to see if William was watching me in the rearview mirror. When we got to school, William helped me out of the car. Then he said, "I'm responsible for you, so be here after school today. I don't want to get into any more trouble on your account, you hear?"

"Okay," I said with a shrug. I didn't feel like going to the mall today anyway. I really didn't feel like seeing anyone today. I walked a different way into school so I didn't have to pass the flagpole where Lori and Maria and the others were.

I walked up the stairs, then across the bridge to the library. Don't ask me why. I sure wasn't going to do any homework. Slipping inside the door, I made a beeline for the back so no one would see Lindsay—or Olivia—at the school library.

I sat down at the table and drummed my fingers on the wood for a minute. Then I got up and asked the librarian for some paper and a pen. Maybe I'd write a letter to Mother. While I waited for her to get the paper and pen for me, my eyes scanned the bulletin board. An announcement caught my eye: Field Trip for all Drama Club Members, it said. I almost turned right away from the bright green notice. After all, I wasn't a drama club member. I don't join clubs. Lindsay's law.

But something made me turn back. It was a field trip to the Merriman Arts Center downtown to see the play *Frozen Dreams*, starring Lillian McClain, the famous actress. I'd gotten to see her once at this movie premiere party my mom and stepdad had taken me to. She was beautiful. She even had a whole line of makeup and a perfume named after her. There was just something special about her.

I breathed in sharply. Ms. Estrada saw me looking at the paper.

"Wow," she said. "Can you imagine getting to see Lillian McClain? Those drama club kids are in for a treat," she said. Then she looked at me. "I guess kids like you get to see her all the time."

That thought made me laugh. Why would I see her all the time? What did my mother— a game-show hostess—and a great stage actress like Lillian have in common? That librarian sure wasn't very smart. But I smiled and acted like, yeah, I'm a celebrity's daughter. Lillian McClain and I are really tight— practically best friends.

"Well, anyway, can I help you find a particular book?" the librarian asked as she gave me the paper and pen.

Just then, I saw Kevin walk into the library.

Frantically, I tried to think of a reason to be here, other than just hiding out from people.

"Uh, where are your books on horses?" I asked.

"Third shelf to the right."

Leaving the paper and pen at the counter, I walked over to the shelf. Grabbing the first horse book I saw, I sat back at my table and hoped Kevin wouldn't see me. Or maybe I hoped he would see me. When I stole a glance over to where he was, I saw that he was looking straight at me. I lowered my head because I could feel my cheeks heat up. That was weird. I never blushed before. Two seconds later, Kevin was standing next to my chair.

"Okay. I was wrong. Girls like you do go to the library," he said. I laughed and closed my book.

"What are you reading?" he asked, glancing at the book's cover. "You like horses?" he asked.

I studied Kevin's curly black hair and deep blue eyes before answering.

"Yeah, but I've never had one before," I confessed. "I don't really know anything about them."

Kevin's face broke into a gentle smile that I'd never seen before.

"My grandma and grandpa have horses on

their ranch. I've spent a couple of summers there. I'm an okay rider," he said. Then he shook his head. "I wouldn't think a girl like you would like horses."

"I bet a lot of things about me would surprise you," I muttered, thinking about my less-than-perfect family situation. But then I shook off that serious thought. After all, Kevin was being nice. I ought to be nice, too. "I surprised you about the library, too. Do you think I'm just a party girl?" I asked.

Oops, did he think I was hinting about his party?

"No, I don't think you're just a party girl," Kevin said. I guess he didn't take my question as a hint. He brushed his hair out of his eyes. Then he gave me a wickedly cute grin. "But, Lindsay, you have to admit, you are hard to figure out sometimes."

Olivia would have tossed back some smart-aleck remark. But Lindsay just smiled. And it was Lindsay that Kevin was noticing right now—noticing in a good way. And not noticing because I was a star's daughter.

"Hey, Kevin," I said suddenly, "You're in drama club, aren't you? Do you think I could join? I want...I want to see Lillian McClain."

"I don't see why not," Kevin replied. "See Mr. Moseley about it."

The bell for first period rang just then.

"See you in drama class. You know, we have to get together and work on our scene. I think we'll be pretty good together." Kevin put his hand on my shoulder and squeezed it, then walked off.

I sat in my chair, that squeeze sending a weird sensation through me. *We'll be pretty good together,* Kevin had said. Okay, okay, so he meant we'd do well in our scene together. But I jumped out of my seat and went over to check out my horse book, feeling happier than I had felt in days.

Mr. Moseley seemed pleased when I asked him if I could sign up for drama club. He gave me a permission slip for the field trip.

"So, you like Lillian McClain too," he said. "She's best known for her movies and her cosmetics line, but you haven't seen her talent until you've seen her on the stage. She's fabulous."

Mr. Moseley led our class to the auditorium. The class paired off in groups to work on the scenes. Kevin and I found seats near the back of the auditorium where we could work undisturbed. Most of the other kids headed up front and some went on the stage.

"I want to keep ours quiet until we actually perform it for the class," Kevin said. "It'll be better that way—more dramatic."

"You take this acting stuff seriously," I said.

"So do you. You just pretend you don't," Kevin shot back. But he was smiling.

I shrugged and sat down, tucking my legs up under me. Pulling my playbook out of my purse, I opened the book to *The Lady and the Pirate*.

We tossed our lines around for a while. It was hard for me to concentrate on the dialogue though. I kept thinking about my mom partying it up in Paris. Then from time to time, I'd start looking at Kevin and seeing a gorgeous, curly-haired guy instead of a pirate. I kept missing my cues.

Finally Kevin slapped his book down on his knee.

"Lindsay," he said. "You're not paying attention. You keep messing up. What's your problem?"

"Don't start fighting with me," I said. I knew it was my fault I was flubbing up. I couldn't keep my mind on the scene.

"We don't have much time to practice. I need a good grade, and so do you." Kevin glared at me.

"I don't care about grades," I muttered.

"Well, I do. Let's try again." Kevin sighed as he picked up his book.

"How long do you mean to keep me captive, you villain?" I read smoothly from my book. I tossed back my head and tried to look brave and defiant, the way Lady Veronica would.

The pirate looked at me and laughed wickedly. "As long as I want to, fair lady," he said. Then he stopped.

"You know, it's none of my business, but it would be better if you didn't wear those tough black clothes when we work on this. It's hard to see you as a fair maiden in that get-up. Maybe you could wear something a little softer."

That was it! Kevin might be cute, but he wasn't going to tell me how to dress. I jumped up and threw my book on the floor. "This isn't the dress rehearsal for a play at the Merriman Center, in case you didn't know it. And no one tells me what to wear!" I said hotly. "I happen to like how I'm dressed!"

I suddenly felt the class looking at us. I looked over and Mr. Moseley was watching us too, shaking his head slowly.

"Can't you two ever stop this nonsense?" he asked.

"I'm sorry, Lindsay," Kevin said after a minute. He started picking at imaginary lint on his dark blue sweater.

Even though I knew I was partly responsible, I didn't apologize back. I was too angry. Whenever I let people close to me—even just a little—they started to think they had the right to run my life.

Kevin and I didn't speak to each other for the rest of the class. When the bell rang, I sprang out of my seat and sprinted out the door. I skipped up the stairs two at a time and shoved my playbook in my locker. Then I walked down the hall the back way so I could avoid everybody.

As I got to the top of the back stairs, I noticed a trash can that was sitting there. Grabbing it, I tilted it on its metal side and kicked it down the stairs. I could hear it rattling and bumping all the way to the bottom of the stairs. I took off down the hall in the opposite direction, my own frustration rattling around in my brain.

It was time to hit the mall again and hang out with my new friends. They didn't criticize the way I dressed. And they'd never get close enough to hurt my feelings.

Six

AS soon as I got to the mall, I cruised for a while, looking for Robbie, J.J., and Lisa. I went into the music store and bought a couple of tapes. I left and went to the card store, where I bought a funny card to send to Alfred. Finally, I spotted Robbie, J.J., and Lisa hanging out in front of the video arcade.

"Oh, you're here," said J.J. She was chewing this huge wad of purple gum, blowing bubbles and cracking the gum loudly. Today she was wearing earrings shaped like spiders. "We just got thrown out of this stupid place."

"'You girls got no money, you get outta here,'" Robbie imitated the arcade manager.

I laughed, because I figured that was what they wanted me to do.

"Well, now what?" J.J. asked, looking my outfit up and down. "Nice clothes," she added. The other girls looked at me, like they were expecting me to drum up something to do. I glanced at the stores.

"I don't have any money," I said.

"No money? No problem!" J.J. said, snapping her fingers. The others laughed again. Lisa walked over to an imaginary counter and pretended to swipe something off it.

"Let's go," said Robbie gleefully. "I'm ready."

"Ready for what?" I asked, even though I had a good idea what they were ready for.

"Ready for what, the good girl asks," J.J. said, mimicking me. I don't like it when people make fun of me. Lindsay's law. I gave J.J. my best icy, cold stare. J.J. didn't look away.

I'd read once that when a wolf looked into the eyes of the leader of the wolf pack, he was challenging the leader. And when the challenger didn't look away, the next step was a showdown. Something made me look down at my shoes.

"Borrowing," Lisa said. "Borrowing stuff from the store permanently."

"But that's shoplifting—" I began.

"We call it borrowing," said Lisa. "What's the matter? You wimping out?"

"No, but it'll just have to be some other time. I—I have to go somewhere today," I said, edging away from the group.

I cut out of the mall in a hurry and started out on the long walk home. I'd only gone a block when I saw our gray limo pull up next to me.

William glared at me as he got out of the car. "Lindsay, I thought we agreed that I would pick you up at school where you were supposed to be." He opened the door for me, and I climbed in the back.

"I...forgot," I said. And the thing was, I really did forget. I looked down and started chipping at my nail polish.

William climbed in the driver's seat, but made no move to start the car. "Tell me what's wrong, Lindsay," he said.

I watched the back of his gray head for a minute, but didn't talk. What was I supposed to say anyway? Instead, I started crying.

"Okay, cry for a bit. Then dry your tears, and you'd better start talking. Where does all this sneaking around get you anyway?" William asked softly.

"What do you know?" I snapped, wiping my eyes with my sleeve.

"Well, my job is being a driver," he answered. "But I'm also a father, you know," he said. "I know when kids are feeling bad and try to lash out at everybody because of their troubles. That's what you're doing."

I fiddled around with the flower holder mounted on the door and thought about that for a minute. "Okay," I said. "So I've got a rich and famous mother, and I live in a big mansion. So I'm a spoiled brat and shouldn't feel sorry for myself," I said. "There. Is that what you want?"

William turned around and hooked his arm over his seat. He took his hat off and scratched his head.

"You've got the right to feel sad when something bad happens to you," he said. "But Lindsay, now's the time when you've got to stick with the winners—the people who care about you. And school's a place where you can go to succeed in life. Especially now—you don't have time for secrets and things that will harm you."

Did William know about my new friends at the mall? All the way home I wondered if he knew.

The next day, I hung out with Lori and Maria between classes. I saw that they were wearing sock charms. In fact, almost half the girls in the eighth grade were wearing them. Lori's boyfriend, Jason Johansen, told her he thought they looked dumb. But after glancing at me, she told him that he didn't know anything about fashion. That afternoon, I waited in front of the school for William instead of heading for the mall.

"There's a surprise for you at home," he said, his eyes twinkling when I got into the car.

"What is it?" I asked, sitting straight up.

"I'm not telling," he said. We took off.

On the way home, I saw Lisa Halloran walking down the sidewalk, her head stuck in a book. Her hair had fallen forward and you could hardly see her face.

"Stop and offer her a ride," I said suddenly. I don't know why. William gave me a look, then nodded. He stopped the car.

I pressed the button and lowered my window. "Hi, Lisa. Do you want a ride?" I asked. She'd probably say no. But at least I was asking.

She smiled and closed her book. Then she nodded.

"Okay. Thanks. Ash was supposed to pick me up and take me to the Youth Club. I don't know where he is," Lisa said.

When she got in the car, she balanced her book on her knees and looked around.

"What are you reading?" I asked.

"It's called *The Mystery of the Swamp*," she said. She looked kind of embarrassed. That was one thing I remembered about Lisa. She loved to read mysteries.

"I'm reading a book about horses," I replied, so she wouldn't feel weird around me.

"I thought you didn't like to read," she said.

"Only some things," I answered.

"I like horses, too," Lisa said.

We didn't say anything for a while, even though I had a bunch of questions I wanted to ask her. Like, did she hate me after what had happened a few weeks ago when I dumped her? And did Ash, her big brother, hate me?

"Want to use the phone?" I asked, just for something to say.

"Okay," she said. "I'll call my mom and tell her I'm on my way over." She picked up the car phone and punched in the number. "This is fun," she said, her eyes sparkling. Then she started talking to her mom.

I shook my head. Car phones were definitely no biggie to me. It was funny how to another person they were a major big deal.

"Bye, Mom," Lisa said, hanging up. "She says hi, and why don't you come, too. Today's pottery day. You could make a clay pot for your mom or something." She was looking at me, waiting for my answer.

Lisa's mom is the director of the Youth Club. They do arts and crafts after school for kids. It's not my thing.

"I can't come today," I said. "I have to get home. There's a present waiting for me. From my mom. She's in Paris," I added.

"My mom never goes anywhere," Lisa said. She sounded almost jealous that her mom never flew off to Paris—dumb, huh?

We dropped Lisa off in front of the Youth Club. Lisa's mom came up to the car and leaned her head in. I could see a dab of whitish clay on her cheek.

"Hi, Lindsay. It's good to see you again. Thanks for bringing Lisa," she said. She sounded like she meant it—not like she hated me for being so mean to her daughter a few weeks ago.

"There you are, Ash," Lisa said. "You were supposed to pick me up."

Her big brother was the star of Grover High's gymnastics team. I used to have a killer crush on him a while back. I mean, he's a total babe. But, I don't know. I guess pretty soon I began to see him like a big brother and...well, you know the rest.

"Hi," I said shyly to him.

His face broke out in a grin. "Lindsay. How's it going?" he asked. He reached over and gave me a high five.

"Okay," I said, pulling my hand back in my window. "Well, I'll see you guys later."

We pulled away from the curb, and I settled down into my seat.

"They seem like nice folks," William said.

"Yeah. They are," I mumbled. Ugh, I was getting that feeling again. Why was Lisa so lucky? Why did she have the perfect family? I could feel tears in my eyes.

As soon as we got to the house, I scrambled out of the car and ran inside to see my present. Just inside the front door was a life-sized stuffed panda bear with a giant, powder blue bow tied at its neck. The card said, *To Lindsay. I'll be home in a few weeks. Love, Mother.*

A bear. I wished the present had been that Mother was home. I lugged the bear up the stairs and set it in my room. Then I cried and missed my mom for the rest of the evening.

* * * * *

Before I knew it, a week had passed. It was the day of our field trip to see the matinee of *Frozen Dreams*. We were gathered in the auditorium waiting for the bus to take us downtown to the Merriman Center. Someone cracked his gum loudly.

"Lindsay, toss the gum, please," Mr. Moseley said without even looking at me.

"It wasn't me!" I protested. How come any time anyone did something wrong, people automatically assumed it was me?

"Sorry, it was me," Kevin said from the seat behind me.

I turned around in time to see him spit his gum into his hand. He winked at me, and I turned around again, shaking my head.

We lined up outside and got onto the bus. I made my way to the back of the bus and sat down. Kevin came and sat beside me. I turned toward the window and smiled so Kevin wouldn't see how happy I was he was sitting with me. This was great. I made up my mind that nothing was going to spoil my day. I wouldn't argue with Kevin no matter what.

Once we got to the center, we lined up and walked in the entrance. There were all kinds of glittery ladies standing around talking in the lobby.

"Check it out," said a girl behind me pointing to a lady with a bunch of diamonds on her fingers.

Some of the other kids were going bonkers over the huge crystal chandeliers and climbing over the red velvet ropes to look out the big windows overlooking the fountains.

"We're heading toward our seats now, ladies and gentlemen," Mr. Moseley said. An usher handed us each a program as we filed in to take our seats. Kevin saved a seat for me right next to him. I sat down and felt very elegant. It was funny. I'd been to lots of celebrity parties and stuff with my mom and stepdad. But today, for the first time, I felt sophisticated coming to a place like this without my mom.

"Are you coming to the drama club party next week?" Kevin whispered to me.

I froze for a second. Was Kevin asking me to his party? I shrugged and tried to pretend it was no biggie.

"Maybe," I said. I tossed back my hair and played with my earring for a second.

"I hope you do," Kevin said. "It's the night after we do our scene. So we'll have something to celebrate."

I tingled down to my knees and back again. Then I pretended to read my program. I guessed it was sort of like he was asking me to come to the party.

"Shhh. The lights are going down," some-one said.

Another kind of tingle went through me as the theater darkened and the orchestra started playing. I loved it right before the cur-tain went up. You could practically feel the whole audience hold its breath, waiting, waiting, waiting. The music swelled and the curtain slowly opened.

The stage was pitch black. Suddenly, a lone spotlight shone and Lillian McClain came walking into it from stage right. The audience clapped loudly. Lillian acknowledged the applause by standing perfectly still and letting it wash over her. Yet it didn't touch her. It seemed like she was sucking all that energy inside her. And then *Frozen Dreams* started.

I'm not sure I even breathed during the whole performance. Lillian McClain was...well, awesome. There was no other word for it. My eyes didn't leave the stage for a moment. She got three standing ovations when the play was over. I clapped my hands off until Kevin poked me in the side.

"Come on, are you starstruck or what?" Kevin asked with a laugh.

"I am not starstruck," I snapped as we started up the aisle.

As we walked up the aisle, I heard Mr. Moseley talking to someone. "Stage acting. Now that takes skill."

We climbed back on the bus. All the way home, I could hardly talk. I was still thinking about the play...and Lillian.

When we got back to school, Mr. Moseley came over to me. "I'm glad you came with us to see that, Lindsay," he said. "That could be you one day, maybe."

Usually, I can take things like that without a second thought. People were always saying stuff about how I was going to follow in my mother's footsteps and be a TV star too. I usually smiled and said, "Maybe." But this was different. I'd never felt the way I felt when I saw Lillian on that stage during all those times I sat out on the set of *Treasure Trove* and watched my mother. And it was scary.

"YAWN," I said in answer so Mr. Moseley wouldn't know that Lillian's performance had gotten to me.

And all of the sudden I wanted to get home. I wanted to talk to my mom. I wanted to tell her about Lillian McClain. And I wanted to ask her if she was so talented, why she wasn't on the stage. Why was she throwing away her talent being a game-show hostess? The minute I got home, I charged up to my room to call my mom. I didn't even stop to think what time it was in Paris.

"Hi, Mother?" I said into the phone as soon as it was answered.

"Hello. Who's this?" My mother's voice sounded sleepy.

"It's me, Lindsay," I said.

"What happened to Olivia?" Mother asked.

I was surprised she remembered that. "Never mind that, Mother," I said. "Guess what? I just got back from a drama club field trip."

"I didn't know you joined the drama club," Mother said. She's been trying to get me to join the drama club ever since I started Foothill Middle School.

"Well, I joined so I could go on this field trip," I said. "Anyway, we saw Lillian McClain in *Frozen Dreams*, and you wouldn't believe it. Mother, it was awesome. Remember, we met her once? Anyway, Mr. Moseley said that that could be me one day. Weird, huh?"

Mother didn't answer at first. "Yes," she finally said.

Had I said something wrong? She was the one who was always bugging me to be in drama class and everything.

"What's your prob?" I asked, getting mad and kicking Panda off my bed.

"Don't talk to me in that tone of voice, young lady," Mother said. "It's just that...well, did you know Lillian McClain and I were roommates in New York a long time ago and...oh, never mind. I've got to go."

Stunned, I listened as the phone on her end clicked in the receiver. She had hung up on me!

I threw my phone onto the floor and stomped out of my room. I started down our staircase just as Sheila started up.

"What's wrong?" she asked.

"Oh, nothing," I shouted. "It's no big deal. My parents are separating. My mother hangs up on me when I call her. My whole life is falling apart. Really, it's no biggie."

I yanked open the front door and stalked out toward Princess' stall.

Seven

UGH—a whole weekend stretched before me, and I had nothing to do—a big fat zero. The thought of moping around our big old house was too depressing. There wasn't a single thing to do.

Usually Mother took me shopping on Rodeo Drive on weekends. Or sometimes, we went to big fancy birthday parties for some stars' kids. They'd put up huge, striped tents on the lawns of someone's house or decorate a set at a studio. I'd hang around and dance, or go talk with the band members. Once, I goofed around with some kids from *What's Up?*, that TV sitcom you hear so much about. We all started throwing pretzels at the DJ's who were doing the music. Mother went totally nutzoid and made William come to pick me up early. But she didn't ground me. She never grounds me.

Anyway, there was a party this weekend that I'd been invited to with Mother. Mother had said I could go without her if Sheila would come. But I didn't want to go. It was for Jared Henderson. He's the cute kid on a soap opera called *With All My Heart*. Personally, I think he's a conceited dweeb. Anyway, the last thing I felt like doing was going to a celebrity party and seeing all those boring people.

I picked up my tennis racket and looked at it. But then I threw the racket down. The idea of hitting around a tennis ball by myself seemed totally bo-RING.

Suddenly the phone rang. I pounced on it. At this point, I was so lonely, I'd talk even if it was one of those computer recordings trying to sell us something.

"Can I speak to Lindsay, please?" It was no computer salesman. It was Kevin!

"This is me," I said, cradling the phone under my ear. I sat down on my desk with my feet resting on the chair.

"Hi. What're you doing?" he asked. Was it my imagination—or did he sound bored out of his socks too?

"Nothing. It's a big yawn around here," I said.

"What? No parties? No movie premieres or whatever it is you movie-star types do?" he asked, teasing me.

I laughed. "No. Just one party. For Jared Henderson."

"*The* Jared Henderson? As in *With All My Heart?*"

"Uh—" I suddenly realized how conceited that sounded. "No, I was just kidding. No parties. I was just going to go hit some tennis balls around."

"Well, um, Lindsay, do you want to go horseback riding with me and some of my friends today?" Kevin asked.

I toyed around with the phone cord, but didn't answer. I was totally zoided out. Kevin was asking me to do something!

"We're going to rent some horses at the Oaks stables. Do you want to come? My dad's driving."

"Uh, well sure," I said coolly, even though my heart was beating like a drum machine on a rap record.

"That's great," Kevin said. "Um, I better warn you. It's not a very fancy place."

"Oh, stop it," I said. There it was again. People always assumed I was stuck up and had to have only the best. Why couldn't people see I was normal? Oh, well. Kevin had asked me to go. That was all that mattered.

"I have to ask Sheila first," I added.

"Who's Sheila?" Kevin asked.

"My mai—my mother's housekeeper," I said quickly.

"Oh," replied Kevin.

I set down the phone while I buzzed Sheila. She said it was okay to go.

"All right!" Kevin exclaimed. "We'll pick you up in an hour."

I hung up and jumped in the shower. I used some floral soap I swiped from Mother's shower. Then I towel-dried my hair and put on some mascara and lip gloss. I was going to put on some blush, but something told me Kevin was the type of guy who didn't like girls to overdo their makeup. I began digging around in my closet. I found some western boots and a belt I'd worn to a party last year. Then I slid on some jeans and a blue denim shirt.

"You look very nice, Miss," Sheila said, coming into my room with a stack of fresh laundry.

"Thanks," I breathed. I really hoped Kevin would think so, too.

I looked out my window just in time to see a blue car pull up to our gate. I saw Kevin jump out and walk over to buzz in.

I opened the window and called "I'm coming!" I didn't want him to come up to the house. Then he would have really been weirded out.

"Wow! This is some house. Is your family the only one who lives here?" Kevin asked when I came down the driveway and met him at the gate.

I nodded. "Except for the staff, you know—gardeners and some maids and our house-keep—oh, never mind. Let's not talk about it," I said.

"Okay," Kevin said, running his hand through his thick, dark hair. As we walked through the gate I turned around and waved at Sheila, who was standing in the front doorway with Duke.

Kevin introduced me to the kids in the car. "Gabe Samuels, Todd McGuire, Luke Ortega, and his sister Kristen," Kevin said.

I didn't know any of the kids. That made me feel a little shy. But I told myself that here was a chance to do normal stuff with normal kids, and I'd better make the most of it.

"Dad, this is Lindsay," Kevin said.

"Nice to meet you, Lindsay," Kevin's dad said. He looked just like Kevin, with dark hair and blue eyes. I liked him right away.

"Do you like to ride horses?" Kristen asked me. She seemed very nice, but I could tell she was sizing up the star's daughter.

"Yeah," I said, trying to shake off that feeling. "I've taken some lessons, but I haven't ridden for a while. This'll be really fun."

"Is your mother really Desiree Sparks?" Kristen asked.

"Uh, yeah," I mumbled, wishing we could get on another subject.

Kevin changed the subject right away. I was grateful. "Maybe since you've taken some lessons, Lindsay, you can give us some pointers," he said. "I've never taken lessons. I just try to hang on the best I can."

"And sometimes he does hang on," Luke added. "But usually he doesn't." We all laughed and nobody talked about Desiree Sparks again. I told Kevin thanks with my eyes.

When we got to Oaks stables, we piled out of the car. Kevin was right. It wasn't anything like the stable I'd taken lessons at. It was old and half falling down. But it was comfortable. And the horses saddled up in the corral looked well cared for.

"I'll pick you kids up in a couple of hours," Kevin's dad said. "Then we'll get something to eat."

This all seemed so normal. Not like my family. Or what was left of it.

While Kevin bought the tickets, I stood next to the barn door and smelled the horses, leather, and alfalfa hay. I scratched the nearest horse. It was an old, white pony who was snuffling me for a treat.

"I like horses better than anything. Even boys," Kristen said, looking at me. "Do you like Kevin?"

I shrugged. "He's all right," I answered.

Pretty soon, this old cowboy-looking guy brought out our horses. Kevin got a big bay horse. They gave the others some sturdy-looking buckskin ones. And I got a pretty, black mare with white socks.

"This is Fair Lady," the cowboy said, giving me a boost up in the saddle. "She's a sweet goer, so treat her right."

"I will," I said, adjusting my stirrups and smiling. The mare felt light under me. I reached over and patted her sleek neck.

Kevin rode up next to me and smiled. "She's a nice-looking horse," he said.

"Kevin, thanks a lot for asking me," I said. I suddenly felt shy, a feeling that hardly ever happened to me.

"I'm glad you could come," Kevin muttered, looking embarrassed and cute at the same time.

We rode for an hour, mostly in a group, but

sometimes two by two on the trail. Sometimes we galloped, but mostly we walked and trotted. I was in heaven. Kevin and I hardly talked, but we didn't need to. It was enough to ride and just be with him and his friends. I was sorry when it was time to turn the horses back for the stable. And sorriest of all when Kevin's dad dropped me back home after we'd stopped off at Taco Treat for lunch.

Walking up our driveway after I'd waved good-bye to everyone, I suddenly felt an overwhelming loneliness. Now I was back to where I'd started from—the rest of the weekend with nothing to do. What was worse was that I'd felt normal for a while, which made my emptiness even more unbearable. I wished for the bezillionth time that Mother would come home. And that she and Alfred would get back together and we could try to be a semi-normal family again.

"Hi, Sheila. I'm back," I announced as I walked in the side door. I let the door slam.

"Did you have a nice time?" she asked, poking her head through the kitchen door.

"It was great. My horse was named Fair Lady, and she was so good," I said. I walked into the kitchen and sat down.

Sheila poured me a glass of juice and set a plate of cookies in front of me.

"Then why do you seem so down?" she asked.

I didn't answer. "Fair Lady was black and she had white socks."

"You really like horses, don't you?" Sheila asked, sitting down at the table. She'd made a cup of her favorite cinnamon tea for herself.

I shrugged. "Yeah. Uh, Sheila, did Mother call?"

Sheila pushed a hair back in her brown and gray bun. She shook her head and stirred her tea.

"No. But maybe she'll call tonight."

"If she's not too busy partying or whatever," I said. I bit off a chunk of cookie forcefully.

"Lindsay, you know your mother really loves you. She's just going through a difficult time now," she said, looking into my eyes.

I looked away. "Well, what about me? I'm going through a difficult time now too, you know."

Sheila sipped her tea, but didn't say anything. I sat there and got madder and madder. Finally, I gulped down my juice, then got up and buzzed for William.

"William, I want to go to the mall," I said. "Be ready in five minutes."

"Oh, Lindsay, haven't you had enough of

that place lately?" Sheila asked.

"No, I like it there," I snapped and walked upstairs to put on my black clothes. I felt like Clark Kent changing into Superman in a phone booth. A few minutes later, I came downstairs, then walked out front and waited for William.

"Lindsay, do you really think you should wear that scorpion necklace?" Sheila asked, following me outside.

I didn't answer, I just marched out to the car and got in.

"Don't charge anything!" Sheila warned. I rolled up the window to shut out the sound of her voice. Then I rolled up the glass partition so I didn't have to talk to William either.

I made William drop me off at the far end of the parking lot so J.J. and the others wouldn't see me getting out of a limo. I walked in, and passed the sock store. It was pretty crowded, but I didn't see them anywhere. I walked over to the music store and went inside.

"Can I help you?" a salesguy with an earring asked me.

I shrugged and looked around for my friends. "Uh, what's playing right now?"

"That's the new album by the Fabulous

Toad Lungs. Like it?" he asked.

"Yeah," I said, wishing I could use my charge cards to buy the tape since I didn't have any money with me. I left the store and walked toward the food court. The girls weren't there either. I was about to give up and call William to come pick me up, but suddenly I saw them. J.J., followed by Lisa and Robbie, dashed out of a department store. They ran down the aisle toward me.

"Hey, Olivia!" shouted J.J. She kept running by me. "Come on."

Lisa ran by me and grabbed my arm. "We've got to get out of here."

I turned and followed them around the corner and down the escalator. "Who are we running from?" I gasped as I ran along.

"Quick. Duck in here!" hissed J.J. as she slipped in this little vitamin store. The others followed.

"They'll never think to look for us here," shrieked Lisa.

"What's this all about?" I whispered.

J.J. gave me a cool glance. "We almost got snagged."

"Snagged? For what?" I asked.

"This," said Lisa, pulling a handful of earrings on cards out of her jacket pocket.

"And this," Robbie added. She had two costume jewelry pins in her hand.

I took one of the pins out of her hand. It was cute—a silvery zigzag thing that would look perfect with my denim jacket.

"You like that? You can have it," J.J. said.

I handed it back to Robbie and shook my head.

"No thanks. I'll go swipe my own," I said. I hoped they thought I was too proud to take anything from them—instead of too scared to take something that was stolen.

"Girls, I'm going to have to ask you to leave the store if you're not going to buy anything," a saleslady said, coming up behind us.

"No problem. We're not *buying* anything," J.J. said, then laughed as we walked out.

We went around the corner to the door, then ducked outside the mall.

"Well, Good Girl, you know it's your turn next time," Lisa said once we were in the parking lot.

I swallowed hard. Sure, I'd done things I wasn't supposed to before. But shoplifting was something else. For one thing, it was stealing, no matter how you looked at it. And for another, these days kids could get in big trouble for shoplifting. But I looked at my new friends. They were letting me know what the price was for their friendship. I had to do what they did, even if it meant breaking the law.

I took a deep breath. "Yeah, maybe it is my turn," I said recklessly.

After all, if I did get caught, which I probably wouldn't, all that would mean was that Mother would have to come home from Paris to bail me out of trouble!

Eight

BY Sunday morning, I had completely changed my mind. I decided that shoplifting was the stupidest thing I could do. I may get into scrapes here and there, but shoplifting was a serious crime. No way was I going to get involved with that.

I sat around all day in the stable and pretended I was talking to Princess. Then I went to the TV viewing room where I'd turned out all the lights. It was pitch black except for the glow of the TV. I just kept pressing the buttons on the remote control. There was nothing good on the tube. Even the music videos were boring. Finally I picked up a videotape and slipped it in the VCR. It was a taped version of one of the first *Treasure Trove* shows of the season.

I watched my mother flipping around on the set in a red dress. Her jewelry flashed in the

TV cameras and her smile was glittering as always. I could feel my throat choke up when she looked into the camera.

I jumped as the door squeaked and a slice of light came into the room. Looking around, I saw it was only Duke.

"Hi, you big, dumb dog," I said, reaching out as he walked over to me. I scratched his ears for a minute. "Look, there's Mother."

Then the door squeaked again. This time, the lights flashed on. I blinked.

"Lindsay, what are you doing watching TV in the dark? You'll ruin your eyes," said Sheila. "Aren't you supposed to be doing your homework?" she asked, sitting down next to me.

"I don't have any," I said. As usual, I had a stack of homework, but I didn't want to do it.

"Don't give me that line. I know you have some. At the very least, you ought to be working on your drama scene with that nice boy who asked you to go ride horses with him."

"Why should I bother getting good grades in drama? Look where it got Mother," I said as I snapped the freeze-frame button on the VCR. My mother froze as she was pointing to the grand prize of the day—a shocking pink washer and dryer set.

"Your mother's one of the most famous TV personalities in the country," Sheila said. "I'd say it's taken her pretty far. And it buys all those pretty clothes you have and all those nice vacations that you've been on."

I pressed the freeze-frame button again. The show went on and soon a commercial came on. And guess who was doing the selling on that commercial? You've got it, Desiree Sparks. She was telling America why people should feed their dogs Champion Chomp dog food. I rolled my eyes.

"Why couldn't she use her acting talents on the stage and be like Lillian McClain instead of selling people dog food and looking weird on a game show?" I went on.

Sheila shot me a look. "There are a lot of things you don't know, Miss. And maybe it's not my place, but I think you're grown up enough to try to consider other people's feelings besides your own."

I flipped off the TV and stood up, letting the remote control fall on the floor with a loud clatter.

"Where are you going?" Sheila asked.

"To do my homework!" I shot back.

Instead, I went to my room, listened to my stereo and cried myself to sleep. The next morning, I got up and noticed Sheila hadn't laid out my clothes.

"Where are my clothes?" I buzzed her through the intercom.

"Well, Miss, since you don't wear what I select for you, I decided not to waste my time," Sheila replied.

I switched off the intercom. "Fine," I said to myself. "Nobody cares about me."

I slid into some black jeans and a black sweater. I considered putting on my sock charms, but then decided it was time I let the entire eighth grade know that sock charms were now uncool. I cheered up for a second at the thought.

I went down to the kitchen, said nothing to Sheila, and grabbed a croissant off a plate.

"Hey, William, you've got the morning off," I said into the intercom. "I'm taking the scooter today."

"Be careful," he said.

The first thing I did when I got to school was let Lori and Maria know that sock charms were now totally out. By second period, no one was wearing them anymore. I was feeling good. During third period, Ms. Sheldon called me to the office and told me that she'd had it with my sneaking my scooter on the school grounds.

"I'm calling your mother, and we're going

90

to have a little conference about this matter," she said.

Big yawn—so I was in trouble with the principal again. And just let her call my mother in Paris! Maybe she'd hang up on the principal too, like she'd hung up on me. I smiled and thought of my friends at the mall. I bet they'd been called into the principal's office at their school lots of times. I bet they practically lived there—when they weren't at the mall.

Ms. Sheldon excused me, and I went on to drama class. We were meeting in the auditorium again.

"You're late," Kevin whispered to me. The class was broken up into groups to work on our scenes. Kevin, as usual, was sitting in the back of the auditorium.

"Couldn't help it. I was in the principal's office," I said. I walked past him on my way to give Mr. Moseley my tardy slip. When I got back to Kevin, he asked "Where's your playbook?"

But just then Mr. Moseley called to Kevin and me. "Jeremy and Sarah will trade places with you. You two need to practice on the stage today."

Kevin rolled his eyes.

"I'm ready, Mr. Moseley," I said.

Jeremy and Sarah walked up to take over our seats. Kevin gathered up his books reluctantly, and I led the way to the stage. When we got up there, Kevin dropped his books on a riser.

"Oh, come on. Don't make such a big deal out of letting the other kids see us practice," I said. I was all set to be nice to Kevin after the horseback riding on the weekend. But now he was acting weird about this stupid drama class scene. It got on my nerves.

Mr. Moseley was sitting in the front row watching us. I wished he'd watch the other kids instead.

"Where's your playbook?" Kevin asked again.

I shrugged. "I don't know." That was true. I wasn't sure where I left it last. I had other things on my mind.

"Would someone please lend Lindsay a playbook?" Kevin asked loudly.

"Why don't you just announce it over the P.A.?" I snapped. "Look, I'm sorry. I just left it someplace when I was practicing."

Mr. Moseley found me an extra playbook. I opened it up to the first page of our scene.

"You can keep me imprisoned until I'm nothing but bleached bones, but I'll never tell you where the treasure is buried," I read.

"Try to stop reading, Lindsay," Mr. Moseley said. "I want to hear the feeling in your voice."

"We're just practicing," I protested.

Kevin glared at me. "Do as you wish, pretty lady. I have all the time in the world to wait. But ultimately, you'll tell me where that treasure is," the Pirate said.

"In your dreams, dude," I ad-libbed just to get a laugh. I had noticed that some of the kids had stopped working on their scenes and were watching us up on stage.

"That's not your line," Kevin grumbled as the kids laughed.

"Oh, lighten up," I said under the cover of the laughter.

"Never!" I continued. I threw back my head and arms dramatically, and accidentally dropped my book.

Kevin waited while I picked it up and fumbled to find the page again.

"Why didn't you tell me you were really—" I began again, then frowned. This line didn't make sense.

"You're on the wrong page," muttered Kevin. I could see Mr. Moseley shaking his head.

"Well, excuse me," I said in a phony voice, thumbing to find the right page.

Kevin slammed shut his playbook and his eyes were flashing. He stomped to the front of the stage.

"I don't want to do this scene," he said to Mr. Moseley. "I'm sick of this. Lindsay thinks that just because her mom's a big deal she's a big deal, and she can make everyone else miserable. Well, I am not playing her games anymore. I think she's the worst actress around, and I don't care who her mother is."

I just stood there like someone had kicked me in the stomach. I mean, I knew maybe I'd pushed it a bit, but I never expected Kevin to totally freak out.

Mr. Moseley looked first at Kevin, then at me.

"Okay. I'll give you a solo scene or something," he said. "As for you, Lindsay—"

"Who cares about this stupid class anyway?" I shouted. I spun around and walked off the stage and out the side door.

"Now wait a minute, Lindsay—" I heard the teacher say before the door slammed shut.

I took off running, and felt my anger rip through me. It was all my mother's fault. She was the one who got me in that stupid drama class anyway. She was the one who left me in that big old empty house. She was the one who was going to dump my stepdad and mess up our family once again.

I kept running, and without even thinking, I headed away from school and toward the mall. I'd be safe there. I'd be with my new friends. About halfway there, my side began hurting like crazy, so I slowed to a walk. No doubt about it—Olivia had taken over. And she wasn't going to let Lindsay the wimp, Lindsay the good girl, control her anymore.

I marched into the mall and headed straight for the video arcade. My friends would be there. I knew they would. As I passed a large store window, I caught a glimpse of my face. It was bright red and my eyes were flashing.

"Hey, what do you know? It's Olivia," said Robbie as she came out of the video arcade. She was quickly followed by Lisa, J.J., and another tough-looking girl I'd never met.

I tossed back my head and jutted my chin out to let the new girl know I was someone you didn't mess with.

"Hi," I said.

"Lindsay!" I heard someone call. Turning around, I didn't see anyone I knew. There were just a few older women with shopping bags over their arms. All of my friends were in school now anyway. I looked back at my friends. Good. Maybe they hadn't heard. Maybe I had imagined that someone had called my name.

"Who's Lindsay?" asked Robbie, looking around.

"I don't know," I mumbled. Oh, great. Now I was found out. Who'd given me away? I didn't want my new friends to become like all the others, wanting to hang around me just so my mother's glamour would rub off on them. Or maybe they wouldn't want to be friends at all anymore.

"Hey, Olivia, we're gonna show Gina here"— Robbie nodded toward the new girl—"the fine art of borrowing."

J.J. walked over until she was just in front of me.

"Yeah, and Olivia here could probably show you a thing or two about it," she said dangerously. "She says she swipes stuff all the time."

It was a challenge. Plain and simple. I swallowed hard. Then I thought of Kevin and how mad he made me. My empty house. Ms. Sheldon the principal. Desiree Sparks.

"Well, let's go," I said. "I'm ready."

I saw Lisa and Robbie give each other a look.

On the way to Beckham's department store, my mind started whirling. Even though I was acting cool, I was terrified. What if I got caught? What if Desiree couldn't fix it, and

I ended up in jail? Fear—never let it show. Lindsay's law. Make that Olivia's law.

"Uh, people go to jail for this if they get busted," I heard New Girl whisper. Her skin looked pale.

"*If* they get caught," I said with a slow grin. Gina looked at me like I was the most awesome girl she'd seen in a long time. Even Robbie and Lisa were looking at me with new respect. Let me tell you, Olivia was looking fine right now.

So what are you afraid of? I asked myself.

We walked into the department store. Robbie and the others fell back. They stood next to some racks and pretended to be looking at clothes. I turned around. They were watching me.

"What are you waiting for?" asked J.J.'s eyes.

"Be careful of the cameras," whispered Robbie.

My heart started thumping in my chest. I walked over to the costume jewelry counter and started to examine some bolo ties. No, too long and stringy. They'd be hard to hide. Earrings. Yeah, they were just the thing. All I'd have to do was reach over and pick a card off the spinning rack.

My eyes swept up and down the counter

checking out where the salesgirl was. She'd turned her back. I looked around. No one else was looking. Then I looked up at the video surveillance camera overhead. I could see the camera moving slowly back and forth. Right now, the monitor was on the jeans rack where J.J., Gina, Robbie, and Lisa stood.

Ready, set, NOW!

I darted my hand out. Just as my fingers closed on an earring card, a hand clamped on my wrist.

I didn't move my eyes from the hand. I was caught!

Nine

"LINDSAY Sparks!" said a voice right behind me.

When I dared to turn my head and see who it was, I could hardly believe my eyes.

"Mrs.—Mrs. Halloran!" I gasped.

Her eyes met mine. She didn't let go of my hand. I tried to squirm away, but she wouldn't let me.

"Lindsay Sparks," she said again, this time softly, shaking her head.

I looked past her and saw that my friends were gone.

"Leave me alone," I said. "I'm not your daughter."

Mrs. Halloran watched me, like she was trying to decide what to do with me.

"So turn me over to the store security guards," I said.

"I thought it was you by the video arcade.

I wondered why you weren't in school. And who were those kids?" she asked.

"They are—were my friends till you butted in and wrecked it," I said. "Let me go."

Mrs. Halloran shook her head. "Not unless you let me take you for a soda and a talk," she said.

Was she crazy? She'd just caught me shoplifting, and now she was telling me she'd take me for a soda? And I thought I was the one going nutzoid! After a few seconds, though, I nodded my head. I didn't want to stay clamped to the counter all day.

"Since you didn't actually take anything, I don't think I need to turn you over to the authorities," she said, letting go of my hand.

I pulled it away and started rubbing it dramatically, even though it wasn't that sore.

"Come on," Mrs. Halloran ordered. "You promised. I know a place where we can sit down and talk."

I stuck my chin out, in my best bad-girl style, but Mrs. Halloran didn't seem to notice. She turned around like she expected me to follow. I don't know why, but I did. I usually ran away from lectures if I could. For sure, a perfect mother like Lisa's would give me a world-class talking-to.

On the way to the food court, I kept an eye

out for my friends. Zip—they had disappeared. I was really mad. Who was Mrs. Halloran to mess up my new friendships? I had a feeling she did it just to get back at me about Lisa and the way I'd hurt her.

Just then she placed her hand on my shoulder and gave me a gentle push over to the counter at Oh! Egg Roh!lls. Funny, it was actually sort of a friendly push.

She ordered two large colas for us and some egg rolls.

"Here," she said, handing a paper plate to me.

I took the plate, and began to feel like I was in a scene, like in drama. *This can't be happening to me,* I thought. But it *was* happening to me.

Mrs. Halloran led us to a table in the back and sat down in one of the chairs. I sat across from her, but didn't touch my food.

"Okay, when does the lecture begin?" I asked.

"After I eat. My first rule: never lecture on an empty stomach," she said with a smile. She was like a cat who'd caught a mouse and now was toying with it. She was toying with me. No one toys with me. Lindsay's law.

"Very funny," I said.

"You know, Lindsay," she said. "Ever since

Lisa first introduced me to you, I've thought a lot about you."

"About me? Bad things, right? And now here's proof. I'm a rotten person. I was about to swipe something. Not the sort of girl darling Lisa should play with, right?"

"Wrong," Mrs. Halloran said. "I don't think you're rotten. What you were about to *do* was rotten. But I think you're a very special girl. And," she added, "your being special has nothing to do with your mom."

"My mom's in Paris," I said, poking my straw up and down in its plastic lid.

"Because of her TV show?" Lisa's mom asked gently. I looked up into her eyes. They weren't angry eyes. They were, I don't know— concerned.

Tears started filling my eyes. I tried to stop them—really I did. I mean, who wanted to start bawling in front of everybody at Oh! Egg Roh!lls?

"No. She's there—" I stopped myself and looked away. I remembered that gossip-sheet lady and how what I had said ended up in the paper. I looked back at Lisa's mom and said nothing for a minute.

But then I said, "She's there to—to get away because she's separating from my step-dad. She doesn't care anything about me. So she just left me. I'm the only one at home with our housekeeper and chauffeur and—" I couldn't go on. All of Lindsay's laws got up and walked right out of that mall. The tears started. For real.

Lisa's mom let me cry. So I did. A huge, never-seen-before, all-out Lindsay cry-a-thon right in front of everybody at Oh! Egg Roh!lls.

Finally, I started groping for some napkins. I kept yanking them out of the dispenser. And Mrs. Halloran got up and gave me a hug. It was the kind of hug she gave all those little kids who came to the Youth Club. I was sure that Mrs. Halloran had thought I was a creep, too. But the way she was hugging me right now, you'd never know it.

"I'll bet all this is very tough on you," Mrs. Halloran said.

I sniffled a little. Now I was starting to get embarrassed. Olivia the Cool was now Lindsay the Blubbering Mess.

"Yeah, it is," I said after a gulping minute. "And you know the worst part? Everyone expects me to go on being cool and acting like nothing ever gets to me."

"Have you and your mother talked about this?" Mrs. Halloran asked, letting me go.

I shook my head and used one of the napkins to wipe my nose. "She's too busy with her own problems to notice mine. Anyway, she's in Paris," I mumbled.

"There are phones in Paris. And I don't think your mom is ever too busy for your problems. But she can't read your mind. If you act like everything's wonderful, she might not realize what's going on in your head," Mrs. Halloran said. "Mothers are lots of things, but they're not mind readers."

I thought about that for a minute. I guess I really hadn't tried all that hard to talk with Mother. I mean, I'd only called her that one time. And most of the time, I acted like I didn't care. Maybe I was such a good actress that even Desiree thought I didn't care.

Mrs. Halloran's voice cut back into my thoughts. "Sometimes problems are too big to tackle by yourself. Sometimes you need help. You need to talk to an adult. Preferably your mother." Mrs. Halloran watched me for a moment before she went on. "And you can always come to the Youth Club and talk to me. I'm a great listener. I keep confidences. And I care about you."

"Me? Why? I messed up a couple of your rehearsals, just to be mean. And I got Lisa in trouble at school," I admitted.

Mrs. Halloran nodded. "I know. But I still think you're a very special girl. Lisa knows that, too. So does Ash. We've all done things in our lives we're not proud of. But it's not too late to learn from them and get back on the right track."

I picked up an egg roll that was getting cold and stared at it. Mrs. Halloran was being nice and all, but now she was getting into some real touchy stuff.

"But I don't know what the right track is," I said softly. "I mean, here I am, a TV star's daughter. I'm supposed to act happy all the time like my mom does on *Treasure Trove*. I'm supposed to act like nothing ever gets to me. So I do. I act all the time, even though inside, I don't even know who I am."

"Lindsay," Mrs. Halloran said, looking me right in the eye. "Your first job is to stop acting and start being yourself. Start dreaming a little. Then start thinking about how to make your dreams come true. And remember not to get *your* dreams mixed up with what anyone else dreams for you."

I nibbled on my egg roll for a minute and thought about that.

"I guess I've talked a lot," said Mrs. Halloran with a little laugh. She frowned and tipped her soda cup so she could get the last of her ice. "But let me end this by saying that you won't find your dream hanging around in a mall with girls who are going downhill and determined to take you down with them. People who ask you to steal and risk getting in big trouble aren't your friends."

I rolled my eyes. But then I thought of something else.

"It's easy for you to say that. But a girl like Lisa couldn't be my friend either. Her life is perfect. She has you for a mother, a nice dad, a cool big brother. Her life is normal. Not like mine," I muttered.

"I'll drive you home," Mrs. Halloran suddenly said. She got up and cleared the trash off our table.

Ha! I thought. Mrs. Halloran couldn't say anything to that.

But I was wrong. As soon as we got out to the parking lot, she said, "No one's life is perfect, Lindsay. Every family has something it has to tangle with. Take our family—Ash and Lisa fight like cats and dogs. Lisa thinks being an only child would be the most perfect thing in the world. Do you think that's true?"

I couldn't help but laugh.

"See what I mean, Lindsay? She has her family situation. You have your family situation and it's no weirder than anyone else's," Mrs. Halloran said. "Just different."

"I just feel like no one cares most of the time," I said. "Like no one really has any time for me."

"Everyone feels like that sometimes," said Mrs. Halloran gently. "I sure do."

"You do?" I couldn't believe it.

"Of course. I spend my days trying to help other people with their problems. A lot of times when I come home, I feel like no one has the time to help me with my own." She gave me a weird little smile. "You know Lindsay, I think we might have something in common."

"What's that?"

"Well, everyone thinks because I work with people, trying to help them with their problems, that I must have all my problems solved—almost like I shouldn't have anything to complain about. Does that sound like anyone you know?"

I knew right away what she meant. She was like me. Just because everyone thinks my life must be perfect, they think there's something wrong with me because I'm not happy. Well, other people don't know what it's like to be me.

"And Lindsay," she added quietly, "I know another person who might be in the same boat. Someone who seems to have a perfect life, but might not be quite as satisfied as everybody thinks."

I couldn't think who she meant. "Who?"

"Your mother," she said, starting the car.

We were quiet for most of the ride home, and I thought about what she said about Desiree. Could it be true? I realized with a little shock that I really didn't know my mother all that well. I couldn't really say if what Mrs. Halloran said was true or not.

"Are you going to tell my mother on me?" I asked when we stopped outside our gate.

She shook her head. "No. I think you should call her and talk to her about everything you're feeling. And you'll tell her about this afternoon yourself," she said.

As I was getting out of the car, she said, "You know, Lindsay, I always thought there was more to you than all the glitz and show you put on for people. And I suspect there's a lot more to your mother than you ever guessed. Try to get to know her, Lindsay. You might be surprised at what you find. And you just might realize how lucky you are," she said softly to me.

Ten

WHEN I buzzed at the gate, I turned around and waved good-bye to Lisa's mother. Lisa sure was lucky to have a mother like that. But maybe Mrs. Halloran was right. Maybe I was lucky to have Desiree. I just let a lot of other things get in the way.

The buzzer sounded and I walked in and on up our driveway. Boy, I was in for it now. Sheila and Mother had told me not to go to the mall. And now here it was almost supper time, and I'd just come home.

Sheila met me at the front door. But she didn't seem mad. She actually seemed kind of happy. She kept smiling this doofy looking grin, but she didn't say much, just, "Oh, Lindsay. There you are."

I looked at her for a minute, then shrugged. If she wasn't going to climb all over my case, I wasn't going to worry about it. I had enough other stuff to think about. I walked in and went straight into Mother's office.

First thing I was going to do was try to sort out some of my dreams, like Mrs. Halloran said. About a year ago, this famous rock star who was on *Treasure Trove* had shown me a piece of paper he carried around in his wallet. It was like a checklist of things he wanted to do in his life. He'd already checked off stuff like "graduate from college" and "be a rock star." And he'd told me he was going to check off the other things, too. That was the way he went after his dreams. It sounded good to me. Now the only trouble was finding some paper.

I rummaged around in the top desk drawer. No luck. So I checked in the next few until I got to the bottom drawer. I had trouble opening this one. Something seemed to be sticking up in it, making it hard to pull. I gave it a good yank. It was jammed with yellowed newspaper clippings and photos and stuff.

I almost shoved the drawer closed again, but something caught my eye. It was a clipping with the headline, "Sparks Fly As Actress Makes Stage Debut." It was an old article about my mother. I read the article. She'd been the star of a play staged in a theater back east. And there was more. I found at least three programs from other plays she had been in.

It was funny, but I never really knew she'd been on stage. I thought Desiree had gone straight from college or something right onto the set of *Treasure Trove* to give away llamas and washing machines.

But, no. Here was evidence that Desiree had had a very different life before I was born. I wondered what happened. Then I picked up another newspaper clipping that told about two great stage actresses—Desiree Sparks and Lillian McClain!

Mother had mentioned that they had been roommates in New York. Judging from the date on the clipping, it was right before I was born. Then I found a couple of faded color photos of my real dad, whom Desiree had divorced when I was two. But these must have been before I was born too, since I wasn't in either of the pictures.

I knew it was snooping, but I couldn't stop. I kept digging through everything until I found another clipping dated six months after I was born. My eyes raced over the print. It was a column by one of those celebrity-gossip types. The report said, "struggling young actress hits the jackpot in TV game show deal." Desiree had been struggling? Wasn't she doing well as an actress on stage in New York?

I guess not. This article told about the trials and tribulations of a young actress and her husband trying to support a baby—me. And how *Treasure Trove* was the answer to her prayers. She'd given up her life on the stage so she could earn money to take care of me!

Duke came shuffling in just then. He sighed and looked at me.

"Listen to this," I read to Duke: "'Now I can take care of baby Lindsay in the way she deserves,'" says the newest hostess of TV show.

Duke yawned one of those humongous yawns with the whine mixed in.

"Dumb dog," I mumbled, scratching his ears. "Don't you see what this means? Mother gave up her dreams of the stage so she could make a good life for me."

I closed the drawer and sat in Mother's chair and thought about that and a bezillion other things for a while. For a long while. I finally got up and was about to go to my room when Sheila came walking down the hallway.

"Oh, there you are," she said. She still had that same doofy smile on her face.

"Okay," I said. "What's going on?"

"Uh, there's someone coming up the driveway," she said.

I looked out the window and saw our long,

gray car coming through the gate. Behind the car was a horse trailer van. So that was it. That was why Sheila was acting so weird.

"Mom bought me a horse! And you picked it out because she's in Paris!"

"Not exactly," Sheila said.

"What is it then? And what's with the horse trailer?" I asked.

Just then, the buzzer sounded.

"Oh, Lindsay, I'm home." It was Mother's voice! I turned around and ran out of the house.

"Mother! Mother! What are you doing home?" I yelled as I ran up to the car. "I thought you were going to stay in Paris for a lot longer."

"I thought I'd been away from you for too long. Do you know how much I missed you? It was time I came home."

I looked past her at the horse trailer. I was getting a bad feeling again, the same old bad feeling. Mother had done it again. Whenever she thought something was wrong with me, she'd buy me something to make me feel better. Only it never worked.

She saw me looking at the trailer and said, "I got to thinking. You've been mentioning having a horse lately. And I know you've been through a lot..."

I didn't wait to hear the rest. I walked over to the horse trailer, all kinds of emotions jumping around inside me. Sure, I wanted a horse, but somehow, just this once, I kind of wished Mother hadn't run out to buy me anything I wanted.

The driver of the trailer van was letting down the ramp. Looking in, I saw *two* glossy, blond tails and powerful rumps.

Something just snapped when I saw the two horses. My mother was never one to do anything halfway. If one horse was good, buying me two horses would be even better—that must have been what she thought. If Lindsay is really down in the dumps this time, maybe she needs two big presents!

"Well, what do you think?"

The tears started burning at the back of my eyes.

"I can't believe you!" I said between sobs. "You're trying to buy me off again!" I turned and started running. Down the driveway. Out the gate. To where? I didn't know.

I ran and ran, down the boulevard. I found with a shock that I was running toward the mall! My muscles began to ache. My lungs burned as I gasped for breath. Salty tears ran down my face. My mom was back, but I felt more alone than I ever had before.

Suddenly I realized that there was a car following me. I looked around and saw the gray limo. But Mother, not William, was driving. I ran faster. But not fast enough.

I heard the car stop behind me, then I heard the car door open. Then Mother came running up beside me.

"Lindsay, where are you going?" she asked.

I didn't slow down. "I'm going to the mall. What do you care?"

"Lindsay, please," she panted. "I can't run like this!"

"You've been running away from me ever since I can remember."

"Oh, Lindsay," she said. "Is that what you think?"

Then I heard an unbelievable sound. I heard my mother crying. That made me stop running. I looked at her.

"Maybe you're right," she said between sobs and gasps. "Maybe I have been running away. "But never away from you. You have to believe that."

"But you're never there when I need you," I said.

She reached out and put her hand on my shoulder. "I plan to be around a lot more from now on," she said. "I realized a lot of things while I was away. One thing I realized is that

I can't run away from my problems. And neither can you—no one can. We have to face them. And we can do that together."

She lifted my chin so I was looking into her eyes. I jerked away from her.

"Mother, I want to tell you something. I've decided I want to be an actress—a stage actress."

She searched my face for a minute. Then she said, "It will be a lot of hard work. It will take all your energy and heart and talent."

"Yeah? So?" Didn't she think I could do anything?

She looked hurt. "Yeah, so I think you could be a great actress," she said. "I'll help you if you want me to."

"Mother, are you sorry I was born and you had to give up stage acting?" I asked suddenly.

"So you know about it now," she answered. "I was going to tell you the whole story soon. But to answer your question, no. I've never regretted my decision. A long time ago I thought I wanted to be a stage actress, but I know I'm happier doing what I'm doing now. I didn't have what it took to be a stage actress. I also know if I had stayed on the stage, I wouldn't have been a good mother to you."

When she said that, she started to get tears in her eyes. "I'm going to be a better mother to you, Lindsay, I promise. I might be clumsy, and I might not always do the right thing. But I'll always love you. And we have to stick together and work on things together. When it comes down to it, you're all I've really got."

The sight of your mother standing in front of you, crying her eyes out, can really be like a stab in the heart, let me tell you. I broke up and hugged her, right there on the street. I didn't care if all the gossip reporters in the world were standing right there.

After we had a good cry, I said through my sniffles, "Why did you have to go out and buy me two horses? One would have been good enough."

"No, it wouldn't," she answered, drying her eyes with a tissue. Her makeup had run all over the place. "The other horse is for me. We can ride them and take care of them together, every day if you want to." She smiled through her tears.

"That's fantastic," I managed to blubber. Uh-oh—Lindsay's law about public blubbering was broken again!

We walked back to the car with our arms around each other. It was then I noticed that there was a crowd of little kids staring at us. We smiled, all embarrassed.

As we were getting into the car, one little

boy shouted, "Show us the prizes, Desiree!"

We just had to laugh!

Back at the house, I was so excited when the driver backed one of the horses down the ramp. He let me hold the rope. It was definitely the most beautiful horse in the world. But then when he backed the other one down the ramp, I thought that *it* was the most beautiful!

Sheila took a picture of us holding the reins to our new horses. William stood smiling at us.

"It's even better than baseball, isn't it, William?" I called out.

He just laughed and said, "Oh, I don't know about that!"

You know what? Mrs. Halloran was right about me being lucky—in more ways than one!

Eleven

AFTER admiring our new horses for a long time, Desiree and I put them in their stalls for the night. Then we sat on some new bales of hay and talked about everything. About Paris. And about some of the changes that were going to take place in our lives. Sad ones, like the separation from my stepdad. But good ones, too, like how we were going to spend more time together.

And we talked about feelings—my feelings. I told her about the girls at the mall and Mrs. Halloran and the shoplifting. And I didn't even really mind that she grounded me for two weeks. Well, just a little, because that meant I'd miss Kevin's party. But he'd never really asked me anyway. And after yesterday, he'd probably never speak to me again.

"So what are we going to name our two new beauties?" Desiree's voice cut into my thoughts. "I think I'll name mine Guinevere, she said."

I knew right away. "I'm naming my horse Princess."

By the time I climbed the stairs to my bedroom, I was so tired I could have fallen asleep in a second. But as soon as I crawled into bed, I remembered something important. Tomorrow my scene with Kevin was due. Even though Kevin had asked Mr. Moseley to let him out of our scene, I knew that he would really rather be a pirate than do a solo. So I spent the next couple of hours under my covers with a flashlight and my playbook, memorizing my scene.

The next morning, I awoke to find my black jeans and a sweatshirt laid out over my chair. I laughed. Sheila was one step behind. Instead, I put on a pair of checkerboard shorts and a long, white T-shirt that said "Malibu Beach Club." Then I put on my sock charms. I'd decided they were cool again. At the last minute, I threw a lacy blouse and a skirt in my backpack for my part as the Lady. Finally, I grabbed my silver satin jacket that had *Treasure Trove* embroidered across the back. It's the jacket that the cast and crew of the TV show wear.

Tucking my playbook into the waistband of

my shorts, I zipped downstairs. Mother smiled when she saw that I was wearing my *Treasure Trove* jacket.

"I'm glad you're up early," she said. "Let's go for a ride. But you'll have to change into jeans."

"But I'll be late for school."

She looked at her watch. "Not if you hurry."

I bolted upstairs again and changed, then raced to the stable. Mother already had her horse ready to go and was starting on mine. When everything was ready, we mounted our horses and started down the driveway to the bridle trail behind our house.

"Isn't this fantastic?" she asked me after we'd been riding for a time.

"Sure is. How do you know so much about horses?"

"I had a pony when I was a little girl," she answered.

"I didn't know that."

"There are still a few things you don't know about me," she said with a smile.

I laughed. "That's probably true," I answered. "And there are probably some things you don't know about me!"

"Well then," she answered with a big smile. "We've got some catching up to do, don't we?"

Too soon, it was time to head back to the

house. I brushed Princess, then ran into the house to change for school. After a quick breakfast, I hopped on my scooter and rode to school.

I coasted up to my friends at the flagpole.

"You're going to get into trouble again about that scooter," Lori said.

"You're wearing sock charms," Maria said right away, looking down at my feet.

I held up one foot and inspected the creepy creatures crawling around my sock.

"Yeah, I like them."

Lori looked mad. "I threw out my sock charms," she said glumly.

Then I felt kind of bad. I knew she threw them out because she thought I didn't like them anymore. So I bent down and unpinned a few of mine, including my favorite, the iguanas. I gave them to Lori.

"Here. You can borrow some of mine," I said. Lori cheered up and sat down on the sidewalk and put them on.

"I've got to go," I said. "I have to park this thing where Ms. Sheldon won't find it, then go to the library and study," I said.

Both of them looked at me like I'd just grown an extra arm right in front of them.

"Study?" exclaimed Lori. "You?"

I took off laughing. Let them wonder.

I studied my scene in the quiet of the library until the bell rang. I studied in my next few classes every chance I got. Then I changed into my Lady clothes right after second period.

I was the first one at the auditorium for drama class when the bell rang. Only Mr. Moseley was there before me.

"Mr. Moseley, Kevin and I are going to do our scene together after all," I said.

He gave me a funny look, but nodded. "Fine by me," he said.

I acted cool, but inside I was a little nervous. I mean, I had my lines memorized, but would Kevin go along with my plan?

Kevin slid into a seat a few rows behind me when the bell rang. I glanced at him, but he looked away. Had I blown it forever? I suddenly felt sick to my stomach. Maybe I'd done all that studying for nothing. Worse yet, maybe I'd really lost Kevin for a friend. I'd sure been a creep lately—to a lot of people.

Mr. Moseley got up on the stage. "Class, as you know, today I'll start grading the scenes you've been working on for the past few days," he said. "The first team up will be Kevin and Lindsay doing *The Lady and the Pirate*.

You should have seen the look on Kevin's face. If anyone deserved an Oscar for best performance, it was Kevin for his reaction. He got up and smiled at me like yesterday had never happened. Still, you could see he looked kind of worried, probably about me.

But he didn't need to sweat it. I was ready. I stood on stage quietly with my head down, the way I'd seen Lillian McClain do when she stepped on stage at the beginning of *Frozen Dreams*. I pulled all my energy inside and let my nervousness flow out of me. Then I let the character of the Lady take over my body. Then I looked up and tossed off my first line to Kevin. Oops. I mean the Pirate.

It was awesome. Neither of us missed a single cue. You could feel the energy bouncing between us. It didn't matter that there were only a few eighth graders sitting out in the darkened audience and that this was only a drama class at Foothill Middle School. This felt like the stage at the Merriman Center, and Kevin and I were the stars!

When we'd said our last lines, Kevin and I looked at each other with a new understanding. Then we heard wild applause from our classmates.

Suddenly I realized I didn't need a piece of paper to write down my dreams on. The idea was firmly burned into my brain. I was going to be a famous stage actress like Lillian

McClain, and I wasn't going to let anything stand in my way! Lindsay's newest law.

"You two were fabulous," Mr. Moseley said. "But I'm not surprised. I knew if you two would stop arguing long enough, you just might come up with some decent work." Then he shook his head. "I'm proud of you."

Kevin grabbed my hand and gave it a squeeze right in front of everyone. Lightning bolts shot up my arm. Then we walked back to our seats, and Kevin sat next to me.

While the next twosome got up to do their scene, Kevin leaned over to me.

"How did you do that?" he whispered.

"I guess it runs in the family," I said.

"Barf," he said, but he was smiling. "I've been wanting to ask you. Can you come to my party?"

"I really want to, Kevin," I whispered. "But I can't. I'm grounded."

Kevin shook his head. "You're always in trouble. What did you do this time?"

"It's a long story," I answered. "I'll tell you sometime. But I'm not going to do it again. I'm not getting into trouble anymore. There are too many good things I want to do. I haven't got time for the bad stuff."

Just then, the auditorium door opened, and Lisa Halloran walked in. She was carrying a stack of messages. She glanced at me while she walked up to Mr. Moseley. After the teacher took a look at one of the messages, he gave it back to her.

"Lindsay Sparks. You're wanted at the principal's office," he said, shaking his head.

"But I didn't do anything this time," I whispered to Kevin. I got up and followed Lisa out of the auditorium.

"What did I do this time?" I grumbled to Lisa as we started to walk across the quad.

"I don't know," Lisa replied. "I just deliver the messages."

I slapped my forehead with my hand. "Oh no! My scooter. Ms. Sheldon found my scooter! Oh, boy, I'm in for it now. Just when I had decided to be a good girl," I said with a laugh.

Lisa gave me a weird look. I knew she didn't understand what I was talking about.

Outside the office, I turned to her. "Since I can't ride my scooter to school, I guess I'll just have to ride my horse!" I said.

Her eyes grew wide. "Do you have a horse?" she asked.

"Yes," I whispered. "My mother bought two so we could ride together. Mine's a palomino. I named her Princess."

"W—wow!" Lisa stammered. "That's great!"

Then I realized it sounded like I was bragging again. That wasn't what I wanted to do to Lisa. I looked at the ground, trying hard to get out the words I wanted to say.

"Lisa, do you—do you think we could try to be friends again?" I asked. "I know I was a first-class jerk, but I've changed. And I'm sorry for what I did. I really mean it. I want—I want to be friends."

Lisa wrinkled her nose and said, "Big YAWN. You for a friend? Bo-RING." But she was smiling. We walked into the office together where a bunch of counselors, teachers, and students were hanging around.

"Umm, I'm sort of grounded now," I said. "But when I'm ungrounded, do you want to come riding with me? We could have a bo-RING time together."

"Sure, Lindsay. I'd love to go riding," she answered.

I turned around to face Ms. Sheldon. But then I broke another of Lindsay's laws. I ran back to Lisa and gave her a big hug—right in front of everyone!

About the Author

KARLE DICKERSON is the managing editor of a young women's fashion and beauty magazine based in southern California. She lives with her husband and numerous animals, including a horse, a Welsh pony, three cats, a dog, and two hermit crabs.

"I first decided to be a writer when I was 10 years old and had a poem published in the local paper," she says. "I wrote almost every day in a journal from that day on. I still use some of the growing up situations I jotted down then for my novel ideas and magazine articles."

Ms. Dickerson spends her spare time at Stonehouse Farms, a southern California equestrian center she and her husband formed with some friends. She says, "I love to ride my horse around the ranch and people-watch. It seems that is when I come up with some of my best ideas!